DOCTOR IN CHARGE

When Nurse Judith Lidgate returns to her father's practice to help him and his partner, Dr. Renton, she is unaware of the jealousy she has aroused in Heather, their present nurse. Matters deteriorate when Dr. Renton returns from France bringing his attractive young ward, Melanie, to live with him.

DOCTOR IN CHARGE

BY

CLARE CAVENDISH

MILLS & BOON LIMITED
London · Sydney · Toronto

First printed in Great Britain 1977 by
Robert Hale Limited, Clerkenwell House,
Clerkenwell Green, London EC1 0HT

This edition published 1978 by
Mills & Boon Limited, 17–19 Foley Street,
London W1A 1DR

ISBN 0 263 72605 3

Set in 11 on 12pt Baskerville

Made and printed in Great Britain by
C. Nicholls & Company Ltd
The Philips Park Press, Manchester

CHAPTER ONE

"I THINK it went off very well," said the Principal Nursing Officer in a satisfied tone.

The Chief Nursing Officer accepted a cup of tea from the tray proffered by a waitress and sipped it gratefully. "These things usually do."

"There *was* that time when the Gold Medallist fainted just as she appeared on the platform. *Most* unfortunate!"

"It was exceptionally hot that year – I can't think why we always have these functions in the summer – and I believe the poor girl had been ill. This year's winner looked very cool and composed, I thought."

If she could have overheard their conversation, Nurse Lidgate would have been delighted to hear herself thus described. In actual fact, she had felt far from cool and composed beneath the stiff starchiness of her blue-and-white striped uniform.

It was not exactly that she was nervous at having to take her gold medal in front of her colleagues and a large number of parents and friends. But it had been an emotional occasion, the culmination of three years' hard work and the end of a very important and happy phase in her life.

It didn't have to be the end. She had already been offered a job as staff nurse at St. Helen's, and, if she had agreed to stay on, she would have stood a good chance of becoming a sister in a few years' time.

"I think you're crazy," her friend Stella Donaldson had commented frankly. "With so many nurses getting the sack as soon as they qualify, it seems plain daft to throw away the chance of continuing to work here."

"Okay, so I'm daft!" Judith laughed, not at all perturbed at Stella's criticism. "There'll be one more job available for somebody else. And as for nurses finding it hard to get jobs, it's only the swing of the pendulum. In no time at all hospitals will be calling out for nurses and having a recruiting drive in the schools. You know how it goes."

"It's the present I'm interested in just now, Judy, and I don't mind admitting that I was darned glad to be kept on. We can't all win the gold medal and my exam results weren't at all outstanding."

"It was probably easier for me, my father being a doctor. Dad was always ready to explain anything I couldn't understand. He helped me a lot on the medical side and that's always more difficult."

Dr. Rodney Lidgate had been, if possible, even more pleased than his daughter at her success. He came to the prize-giving and applauded loudly when Judith went up to receive her certificate and the medal for being the best all-round nurse of the year.

There was a lump in his throat as he watched her small, misleadingly fragile-looking figure cross the platform. How much her mother would have enjoyed this occasion . . .

"Hullo, Dad!" Judith appeared suddenly before him during the crush which followed as everyone struggled as politely as possible to obtain cups of tea. "Did I look all right? At the last minute I thought my cap was going to slip." She put up her hand and touched the scrap of white lawn balanced on her dark head; because her hair was so short and straight, and fitted her head so closely, she had always had difficulty in getting her cap to remain securely anchored.

"You looked fine to me," her father said. "I was very proud of you and I would have liked to stand on my chair and shout out to everybody that you were my daughter!"

Judith laughed, but he did not join in her amusement. His thoughts were once more of her mother but he did not care to take the risk of putting them into words. Emotion was a very private thing with both of them, avoided whenever possible, and although it was nearly two years since Rosemary Lidgate had died, her loss was still felt keenly.

Judith looked up at his face, noting his unsmiling mouth and the lines round his eyes which did not often deepen into laughter creases. She had not realised how grey he was getting and, although it suited him – since his hair was as thick as her own – it inevitably made him look older.

"Let me get you some tea," she said abruptly. "I'm dying for a cuppa myself."

A few minutes later, refreshed and their feelings well under control, they pushed their way out of the hot marquee, with its smell of crushed grass and cosmetics, and began to walk slowly across the lawn.

"When do you actually leave here?" Rodney asked.

"At the end of the month – in ten days' time."

"You ought to have a holiday before starting your new job."

Judith shook her head. "I don't want one just

now. I'd much rather get my teeth into the job and perhaps fix something up later."

"You must please yourself, of course, but – " He broke off as they were joined by a tall young man in a white coat who had been sauntering to meet them unnoticed by either.

"Hi, Judy!" Sean Hargreaves included her father in his smile. "Hullo, doctor – have you come to share in the glory?"

"I don't know about that, but I'm certainly enjoying it."

"It's a pity Judy's leaving the hospital," Sean went on regretfully and then broke off in some embarrassment. "But I don't suppose you'd agree about that. You must be glad she's joining the group practice."

"Naturally I'm glad."

"Stop talking about me as though I'm not here," Judith commanded. "I've told you my reasons, Sean, and even you could see that they were good ones. It's settled now so don't keep on about it."

"Okay," he agreed cheerfully. "What are you going to do when this free-for-all is over?"

"I'm off duty for the rest of the day. I thought of going home with Dad for the evening."

To Sean it sounded an appallingly dull finish to her day of glory and he said quickly: "How about coming to the disco with me instead? We could have a celebration drink somewhere first and perhaps a meal. I feel like living it up tonight."

Judith was instantly tempted, in spite of the fact that she had spent a good deal of effort during the last few weeks on trying *not* to be alone with him. It wasn't that she didn't like him – in the secrecy of her heart she knew that she could very easily like him far too well – but she quite definitely didn't want to get involved with an emotional tangle just now.

But he was looking at her so yearningly, his blue eyes warm with feeling, that she was tempted to give in. It was, after all, *her* day – as people kept telling her – and she needn't see much of Sean once she had left. A house surgeon didn't get a lot of time off and she would be living six miles away.

"Sounds fun!" She smiled up into his face and had the pleasure of seeing it light up. "If Dad doesn't mind – "

"Of course I don't, dear. You go off and enjoy yourself. I'll have plenty of your company in the near future, I hope."

"I shall be off duty at seven," Sean was beginning when with a rush and a gasp Stella Donaldson erupted into their midst.

"I've been looking for you everywhere, Judy." She broke off to greet Dr. Lidgate hastily, and then returned to what she had been going to say.

"We're fixing up a party at my flat and we want you and Sean to come too. We're all a bit broke as it's getting near the end of the month but we can afford some bottles of plonk, though I'm afraid the eats won't be anything special."

"*Hell!*" Sean's muttered comment reached Judith's ears but Stella only noticed his expression.

"Why on earth are you looking so bad-tempered?" she demanded. "Don't you want to come?"

"We were just – " Judith started to explain but her friend was rushing on.

"You simply *must* come, Judy. You and I have done everything together since our PTS days, and now we've achieved SRN status we've just got to celebrate at the same party."

Judith hesitated, torn between a desire not to hurt Sean's feelings and a suspicion that it might be much more sensible to accept the party invitation.

"What do you think?" she asked.

He half turned away from her with a shrug. "It's up to you."

"We hadn't really fixed it up definitely, Sean, and I'm not leaving the hospital tomorrow, you know. There's loads of time for a farewell drink together. So shall we go to the party this evening?"

Her eyes – as blue as his own but with long dark lashes instead of the thick golden ones which matched his wild corn-coloured hair – gazed up at him appealingly and he was unable to resist.

"Okay." His voice dropped. "But I shan't forget you've promised to come out with me on your own before you go."

"That's fixed, then," Stella said happily. "Around eight at the flat and don't forget to bring a bottle."

As Sean left them abruptly, Judith looked at her watch. "Oughtn't we to be doing some shopping? There's still time."

"I'm only getting bread and cheese and that won't take long so there's no need for you to bother. My parents aren't here so I can dash off now."

When she had gone, Rodney Lidgate – who had been an interested listener – said thoughtfully: "I hope that young man won't spend the evening sulking. I'm afraid he was very disappointed."

"He's not the type – fortunately. Do you think I stood him up too badly, Dad?"

"Not under the circumstances, I suppose. You

would have had to disappoint Stella if you hadn't, and it really boils down the question of which of them means more to you."

There had been a slightly interrogative note in his voice but Judith ignored it. His question was one which she had not yet asked herself; it was more than likely, she felt sure, that she would never ask it.

Having kissed her father goodbye, she returned to to large bedsitting room which she occupied in the block reserved for third year nurses who had not managed to obtain flats for themselves. She was fond of her room, which was attractively furnished and full of personal knick-knacks, and did not at all envy Stella the flat which she shared with her older sister.

As she took off the gold medal she held it up and looked at it almost in awe. She had played it cool among her friends – desperately anxious not to be considered big-headed – but now, alone with her secret thoughts, she had no hesitation in acknowledging that the award meant a tremendous lot to her.

Perhaps it really was rather foolish to give it all up, the wonderful promising future, and go and work as a nurse to a group practice situated in a village. For a brief moment Judith was bitterly resentful because Fate had chosen to deal a shattering blow to the Lidgate family by snatching away a greatly loved mother and wife.

If Rosemary hadn't died so tragically as the result of a rare infection picked up on holiday, Judith would now be free to do what everybody thought she ought to do – stay on at St. Helen's.

But her father needed her at home. He had managed with a series of inefficient housekeepers for too long, and she would find interest and enjoyment in doing both her jobs to the best of her ability. Of that she was quite determined.

Later on, at the party, she forgot all her half acknowledged doubts and gave herself up to gaiety. Sean had, as she had confidently expected, recovered from his annoyance and was now resigned to spending the evening among a crowd.

The gathering was, not at all to her surprise, exactly like every other party she had been to during her three years of training, in spite of being a "special celebration". There was a great deal of medical conversation, in a few cases rather too much drink taken – though not to any serious extent – and a fair amount of pairing off.

Inevitably she was obliged to pair off with Sean, and as the obligation fitted in with her own wish she raised no objection. They had partnered each other at too many parties not to be aware that the "necking" done then could mean as little or as much as the participants wished.

"You're going to miss Sean when you're living in your remote country village," Stella said when they met in the kitchen sink, both of them engaged in procuring fresh glasses.

"There's nothing remote about Bedwell Green!" protested Judith, ignoring the first part of the sentence. "I expect I shall come into Cumberton quite often."

"It won't be the same though, once you've left St. Helen's. I expect you'll soon forget all about everybody here, Sean included. It's obvious that you're not really in love with the poor guy."

Both unable and unwilling to argue about it, Judith said nothing and concentrated on drying a glass on a tea towel so wet that it made her task almost impossible.

"Are there any unmarried doctors in your father's group?" Stella asked.

"One, but I hardly know him. In fact, I think we've only met once – he's new to the practice."

"Maybe he's the one you've been reserving yourself for."

"You do talk a lot of rot," Judith said calmly. "Hugh Renton's perfectly safe from me, I assure you. It wouldn't be much fun for Dad if I started getting romantically involved as soon as I got home."

At that moment several people squeezed into the tiny kitchen, demanding clean glasses, and the subject was dropped. The party ended soon afterwards with the return of Stella's sister, who announced that she would like to go to bed. No one wanted to keep it up very late, in any case, as most of them were on duty early in the morning.

It was her own early duty which made it easy for Judith to ignore Sean's obvious desire to be invited in for coffee after he had taken her home.

"What with one thing and another it's been quite a day," she reminded him, "and I'm beginning to feel a bit shattered. So let's say goodnight quickly, shall we, Sean dear?"

He agreed with the best grace he could muster, but his lingering kiss made her heart beat faster than she could have wished, and he did not leave without reminding her of her promise to go out with him, "just the two of them," before she left.

They met again on the ward in the morning, but since Sean was the youngest and least important member of the surgical team and Judith was not even on escort duty, it was only possible to exchange a smile.

A few days later he managed to snatch a few moments alone with her by following her into the kitchen during one of his routine visits to the ward. Judith turned round from the cooker as he entered and was distressed to find him looking rather troubled.

"Is something wrong?" she asked quickly.

He nodded gloomily. "I've got to go home for the weekend – my father is ill."

"Oh dear, I *am* sorry! Is it – serious?"

"Could be. He's had a stroke and my mother's very worried." He moved a little nearer and looked down at Judith. "I expect I'll be back on Monday or Tuesday, but we'd better leave the fixing of our date until after that, just in case."

"Yes, of course. When are you actually leaving?"

"In an hour's time." He touched her hand fleetingly, but did not risk an embrace.

"I do hope you find your father much better and that it turns out to be quite a mild stroke. The effects sometimes wear off almost completely, I believe."

"That's what I keep telling myself." A faint smile touched his lips and was gone. "See you!"

Judith waved her hand and turned round again just in time to rescue the milk which she had been heating. As she poured it into a beaker her mind was full of the news she had just heard. Poor Sean – he was, she believed, the eldest of several children and there wasn't much money. If anything went wrong, he would have to cope with it all himself.

During the days which followed she looked frequently for his return or – alternatively – hoped for a telephone call from him. But there was no news at all, and nobody seemed to know anything but the bare facts which she already possessed.

It was not until the day on which she was to leave the hospital that she learnt – from another houseman – that Sean's father had indeed had only a mild seizure and was already recovering.

"Sean's staying on for a couple of weeks though, taking some of his annual leave now instead of a bit later on."

He might at least have taken the trouble to let her know, Judith thought rather crossly. It wouldn't have mattered so much if she hadn't been returning home, but perhaps he'd forgotten all about that. Trying to excuse him, she decided that he must have been so completely re-absorbed into his family that St. Helen's had ceased to exist as far as he was concerned.

She shrugged her shoulders over it and went off to do her final packing. The tearing up of the surprisingly strong roots which she had unconsciously put down during the past three years was now so painful that it was a relief when the time came to get into her father's car for the short drive to Bedwell Green.

Neither of them spoke as he negotiated the traffic, and it was not until they were clear of Cumberton that Judith broke the silence with a domestic question.

"I was wondering about the evening meal, whether I ought to have brought something with me."

"It's not your responsibility today," her father said decisively. "Ever since Mrs. Brittain left last week, Heather has been coping with food."

Judith turned a startled face towards him. "I didn't know Mrs. B. had gone, or at least, I didn't think it was so early as last week. Did she just walk out?"

"Something like that," he said evasively, reluctant to discuss his household difficulties now that he believed them to be over.

"But Heather Black is your receptionist and secretary, employed only at the surgery. I hadn't realised that she would ever undertake other duties."

"It's not part of her job, of course, but she's been very good in the various crises which have occurred since – since your mother died. I've owed my main meal to her thoughtfulness more than once, and she's also manned the phone a good deal when I've been out in the evenings. It's very awkward when there's nobody to do that in a doctor's house."

"Yes, of course, but I thought you had the phone switched through to one of the other doctors."

"I do that frequently, particularly when I'm off duty, but sometimes I prefer that the calls should come direct to me."

Judith said no more but at the back of her mind a slight sensation of discomfort lingered. She had known Heather for many years without ever feeling that she knew her at all. She was competent in all she did, and the group practice relied on her tremendously, but her private life was either a mystery or didn't exist at all.

"I hope she's a good cook!" Judith paused and then added honestly: "I don't want her to be too good though, or she'll show up my amateurish efforts."

"You'll manage all right," Rodney said easily. "A girl who can do as well as you've done ought to be able to take a simple thing like cooking in her stride."

His daughter smiled to herself but made no comment, and before long they reached the large straggling village which was called Bedwell Green to distinguish it from Bedwell Market two miles away. The group practice occupied two eighteenth-century houses overlooking the Green, and Rodney Lidgate's house was on the other side of the expanse of rough grass.

Grove Farm House had originally been a Tudor building, but it had been altered so many times during the centuries that it could no longer be assigned to any particular period. Inside it was spacious, and the big kitchen – used a great deal for all sorts of purposes – still retained something of the atmosphere of the farm it had once belonged to, before all the land was bought by a neighbouring farmer.

The door stood wide open and a large bowl of roses on the hall table – arranged by whom? – filled the air with fragrance. Dr. Lidgate was busy with the luggage and Judith stepped in alone, aware as she did so of a more savoury smell filtering through from the kitchen.

As she stood there, looking round and glad of a moment to herself, the telephone in the study began to ring.

Her father was still outside, but as she called out to him: "I'll get it!" the kitchen door opened and a dowdy-looking woman of very uncertain age appeared.

"Shall I? It's probably a patient on the line." She took a step forward.

"I'll have to get used to that, shan't I?" Judith smiled and spoke calmly, but the move she made towards the study was a very definite one. As Heather retreated into the kitchen again, she lifted the receiver and said crisply: "Dr. Lidgate's house. Can I help you?"

But the caller was not a patient. It was Dr. Hugh Renton, and he sounded as though he were in a state of considerable shock.

CHAPTER TWO

"WHO are you? I thought Heather was there –" The voice at the other end broke off abruptly.

"It's Judith Lidgate. I've just – "

"Hugh Renton here," he interrupted. "Is your father available? I must speak to him urgently."

"I'll call him."

Judith laid the receiver down and turned round, to find her father just behind her. As he took over the conversation, she heard an unintelligible murmur from the other end and then Rodney exclaimed in horror:

"*What*? My dear chap, I *am* sorry!"

She had intended to disappear into the kitchen, but the distress in his voice halted her in the doorway of the study, where she remained unashamedly listening. Dr. Renton was obviously terribly upset about something and the one-sided conversation did nothing to alter her conviction that it was a very serious matter.

"Of course you must go at once. Don't worry about anything here, and don't hesitate to stay as long as necessary. What's that? Well, yes, I suppose you'd better let us have a few notes, but I imagine Heather will already know most of it."

There was a brief statement from Hugh Renton and Rodney said: "Very well. We'll expect you in about fifteen minutes."

When the receiver had been replaced, he did not

seem surprised to find Judith still standing there, a look of apprehension on her face.

"Such a shocking thing has happened, Judy. 'Hugh's brother and his wife have both been killed in a coach crash in France. The poor chap's quite beside himself." His own face reflected the horror of the news which he had just heard.

"How *awful* for him! No wonder he sounded in such a state. And how terrible for the parents too."

Her father shook his head doubtfully. "I don't know about the wife, but Hugh and his brother – David, his name is – haven't really got any parents. Their father died when they were quite young and their mother married again and had another family. Eventually she and her second husband went to Australia and I'm not even sure if they still hear from her."

"Were there only the two boys of the first marriage?" Judith asked.

"That's right. Consequently they've always been very close. Hugh will be heartbroken, I should think."

Judith said no more, but the news had cast a shadow over her home-coming. She heard her father in the kitchen talking to Heather and guessed that he was passing on the tragic information which had just reached them. After giving them a few minutes in which to discuss it, she roused herself and went to join them.

The secretary was just taking off a professional-looking white coat, probably one of those used at the surgery. She looked hot, her sallow skin unbecomingly flushed, and Judith wondered – not for the first time – how anyone with such good, neat features could manage always to look so plain. Perhaps it was her hair which – brown and too fine to be easily controlled – she wore in a French roll which did not suit her, and which was invariably untidy.

"Good evening, Judith." Heather had either forgotten or intended to ignore their brief meeting in the hall. "I thought I had better wait until you got here so that I could explain about the meal. Most of it is keeping hot in the bottom of the cooker, but I've only just put the cabbage on as it spoils if it's kept waiting. Will you dish it up or shall I wait a little longer?"

She had said nothing to which anyone could possibly take exception, and yet Judith felt a sense of irritation. She said rather sharply: "Thank you, Heather, but there's no need for you to bother. I can manage." Rather belatedly, she added: "You've done such a lot already. My father says you've helped him a great deal."

"I'm always glad to be of use." Her colour deepening still further, she picked up a fawn cardigan and moved towards the door. "I'll be on my way then."

"Stay and have something with us," Rodney suggested and – finding two surprised faces turned in his direction, went on hurriedly: "It seems only fair after you've done all the work."

Had the secretary been in the habit of staying to share those delicious meals she had cooked so efficiently? Judith wondered, and then dismissed the thought at once. Her father wouldn't be as foolish as that; he'd know how easily tongues were made to wag in a village, and particularly when one of the parties was a doctor.

"It's very kind of you," Heather was saying, "but there's only enough for two, and I have my own meal arranged at home."

She left immediately, and as soon as she was out of earshot, Judith said emphatically: "I'm so glad she didn't stay. It would have been terribly awkward."

"I don't see why."

"That's because you're a man, but you can't have two females sitting down to eat together and neither of them knowing who's supposed to be in charge of the meal. We would have been so polite about it too –we'd probably both have choked."

"What nonsense you talk!" Rodney said tolerantly, and at that moment a ring at the front door recalled to them the tragic news which they had received a sort time before.

Hugh Renton had now got himself well under control. He stepped into the hall and plunged straight into the reason for his visit, giving neither Judith nor her father any opportunity to show sympathy.

"Mrs. Jackson will need a call first thing in the morning. I'm rather worried about her condition – "

As the two men went rapidly through the list, Judith stood in the background, hoping to learn something about the patients and at the same time studying the white, set face of the young doctor.

She could easily recall details of her previous meeting with him. He had been angry about something – a patient, she thought, had made a very trivial and quite unjustified complaint – and her father had soothed him down. His deep-set grey eyes had blazed with annoyance then but there was anguish in them now, and lines of pain on either side of his mouth. The thick chestnut brown hair looked as though he had run his hands through it instead of using a comb, and a lock of it fell over his forehead and was continually being brushed back.

The two men had finished their brief conversation and Rodney said rather formally: "I expect you remember my daughter."

Hugh's gaze passed indifferently over the girl's slight figure. "I knew you had one, of course, but I don't think we've ever met."

"I'm sorry – I thought you had."

"Would you like anything before you go, Dr. Renton?" Judith put in quickly. "A drink, perhaps?"

He shook his head and again made the impatient gesture of pushing back his hair. "I've had one, and I don't think another would be a good idea just now – er – thanks."

Judith did not argue. She had been piqued at his failure to remember meeting her and was angry with herself because of it; after all, she herself had a very clear recollection of the meeting and it wasn't very long ago either. He might at least have pretended, out of politeness.

How small-minded could you get! Judith shook off her irritation and returned to the present. By now the two men had reached the door again and Hugh was on the verge of departure.

"I'll keep you informed," he was saying. "I'll have to go over to France, of course, and I'm not sure how long I shall be there. There are bound to be certain – formalities. But you can rely on me to get back as soon as possible."

Rodney repeated the assurance he had given on the telephone. "Everything will be taken care of at this end and you must on no account feel you've got to hurry. Goodbye, my dear boy, and do be careful. Try to keep your mind on your driving."

When the car had driven away, they went into the kitchen – which was large enough to be used quite comfortably for meals – and began their belated supper. Heather had laid the table in the window and Judith was forced to admit that it looked very attractive, with a small arrangement of sweet peas in the centre. The food was good too and she thought with increased trepidation of how badly her own efforts would compare with it.

Neither of them had much to say as they ate, and Judith at least was having difficulty in controlling her imagination which persisted in picturing Hugh Renton's arrival in France, the difficulties of coping with red tape in a foreign language, the horror of having to identify the bodies.

"Had they any children?" she asked suddenly.

"David Renton and his wife? Only one, I think, but I don't know much about them. I've got a strong impression that they were a good deal older than Hugh, but that's all. He's not been here long, you know."

Judith poured cream over a slice of gooseberry flan and passed the jug to her father. "Has he settled down well in the practice?"

He considered the question, deluging his own helping with cream as he did so. "I think so, but it's early days yet. Country people are slow to accept a newcomer, you know, particularly when he happens to be a doctor. We took him on as an addition too, and that meant people had to be transferred from our three lists to make up his."

"I didn't realise you all had your own patients."

"It's a very fluid arrangement. A patient doesn't always get the doctor he's registered with; he might be off duty, or ill, or busy with an emergency. We all cover for each other, and inevitably some people don't like not seeing the one they've been expecting."

"Do you ever find it a bit awkward being the senior partner in a group practice and yet not the eldest?" Judith asked.

"Not really. John Corder is nearing retirement age and doesn't want to be bothered too much, and poor Andrew Graham would have enough on his plate if he didn't have any patients at all!"

"What on earth do you mean?" Judith got up to fetch the cheese board.

"You'll find out soon enough, I expect. Let's say that he has family difficulties and leave it at that." He broke off and changed the subject. "Heather's excelled herself tonight – this is really a delicious meal."

Judith sighed as she began to collect the used plates. "You're going to be let down badly tomorrow."

Her father caught her hand as she passed, with one of his rare gestures of affection.

"You mustn't talk like that, dear. I'd rather have you getting my meals, and I can't tell you how glad – and grateful – I am that you've decided to come and live at home again. I only hope that being a nurse to the group practice *and* running the house won't prove too much for you."

"Of course not – I'm strong and healthy and I hardly ever get really tired. I'm looking forward to the nursing part very much – it will be quite different to ward work."

"I think you'll find it interesting. You'll have a much closer contact with your patients than is possible, or advisable, in hospital."

"When do you want me to start?" she asked.

"I thought perhaps next week. Laura Heal, the district nurse, is used to managing on her own but there's really too much for her to do now, which is why the practice decided to employ its own nurse to help out."

"I hope she won't mind working with me. It's rather an unusual situation. Do you think I shall have to be very tactful?"

Rodney flung back his head and laughed. "Of course not! Laura is a very nice girl and I'm sure she's looking forward to having your around – not that you'll see very much of her. You'll be helping Heather as well, you know, and that means being responsible for keeping the patients' notes up-to-date."

A look of alarm crossed Judith's face but she did not translate it into words. It certainly sounded as though she would have to tread very carefully indeed if she was not to find herself constantly in the centre of a storm!

They went on discussing her work for some time and she was glad to have it clarified. It turned out that she would have to be handy during morning and evening surgeries, and that she would spend the rest of the morning holding a sort of clinic for patients referred to her by the doctors and whom she could deal with on her own.

"Dressings, injections, cervical smears, ear syringes;

you name it and I can guarantee you'll come across it sooner or later, Judy. You won't be able to complain of monotony!"

She would have the afternoons free, she was glad to discover, though she doubted if she would have much leisure, in spite of having a Mrs. Mayhew from the village to do most of the cleaning at Grove Farm House.

During the next few days she set herself with grim determination to learn all she could about running a house and inevitably coming up against difficulties. Dead flowers on the hall table were easily dealt with but laden raspberry canes presented quite a problem and picking the fruit was incredibly time-consuming.

What did one do with raspberries, apart from eating them raw with cream? Mrs. Mayhew suggested jam or bottling, "or you might persuade the doctor to buy one of these freezers everybody's gone mad about."

But Judith did not think she could cope with learning how to use a freezer just now, and she spent one very hot evening stirring jam which obstinately refused to "jell". Her father declared it was delicious, but since he said the same about everything she cooked – including underdone pastry and dried-up meat – she was unable to accept that he was sincere.

Trying to use her brain as well as her hands, Judith battled on, grimly determined to learn the art of producing well-cooked meals on time – even if nobody turned up to eat them – before she had to add surgery duties to domestic ones.

Her life at St. Helen's Hospital – so recently discarded – now seemed as remote as schooldays had become, and even her friends there had lost some of their reality.

Sean too – she was bound to admit that he too had receded into the background of her mind. He would still be on holiday, she supposed, and no doubt enjoying himself now that his anxiety about his father had been relieved.

Would he get in touch with her when he returned to Cumberton? Or had he decided that it would be better to let their feeling for each other die a natural death?

Of Hugh Renton nothing was heard either, until almost the end of the week when he rang up from London at a time when Judith was alone.

"Will you tell your father that I expect to be back about the middle of next week?" His voice was businesslike and totally lacking in expression. "I'm sorry it can't be sooner, but there's still a good deal to be done."

Judith murmured an appropriate reply, longing to ask how he had been getting on but not liking even to take the liberty of mentioning his loss.

"I'll be getting in touch with Mrs. Crowfield," the doctor went on briskly, "so there's no need for anybody to bother to let her know."

"Mrs. Crowfield?"

"My landlady. I occupy half her house – Birch Cottage, down by the church."

"Oh yes, I know it," Judith said quickly, "but I don't think I've met Mrs. Crowfield. She must have come to the village since I left it to start nursing."

"Probably. Well, I think that's all. Goodbye – er – Judith."

It had been an unsatisfactory conversation and, in

retailing it to her father later that evening, Judith had difficulty in answering his questions.

"How was he? Didn't you even ask him?"

"He didn't give me a chance, and I don't think he wanted to talk about it."

"No, I suppose he wouldn't. I wish he'd been more definite about when he's returning, but I expect it's impossible at this stage."

"Who's Mrs. Crowfield?" Judith asked.

Her father repeated the information she had already received from Hugh, but added also: "She's a teacher at Cumberton High School and I think she finds Birch Cottage a bit big for a woman on her own."

"A widow?"

"Could be, but the general opinion is that she's divorced. She doesn't mix much in village life and consequently gets talked about a good deal. It's an ideal arrangement for Hugh, having half her cottage; she gets his breakfast and evening meal and the rest of the time he fends for himself."

Monday morning came and Judith put on her uniform with a pleasant sense of anticipation. It had been a rush, getting breakfast cleared away and washed up, and the bedrooms tidied before nine o'clock, but she had managed it. Nevertheless, she was glad she had only to walk across the village green to present herself for duty.

Heather Black was in the office, talking to a girl in the blue dress of a district nurse. Her unbecoming cap was perched on top of a mass of reddish hair and she had the pale freckled skin which went with it.

"Do you two girls know each other?" Heather asked conventionally.

Both girls at once denied it, but the district nurse said carelessly: "Don't bother to introduce us – we both know who the other is, even if we've never met. Hullo, Judith – all ready for the fray?" Her bright, greenish eyes flickered over the smart St. Helen's uniform.

"You think there will be a fray, then?" Judith asked with a friendly smile.

"There usually is on Monday mornings. You can't think how many people manage to hurt themselves or develop symptoms during the weekend." She turned to the receptionist. "Who's taking surgery? I hope it's not Dr. Graham, because he's always late and I want to get away."

"It's not his fault," replied Heather. "You know his wife's generally ill and he's got four children."

"You always stand up for the doctors! You wouldn't if you had my job."

"It's my father this morning," Judith put in. "He's making one or two calls but he won't be long."

"Dr. Lidgate is always considerate," Laura Heal acknowledged, "which is more than can be said for Dr. Corder. He's got a wonderful bedside manner, but he thinks nurses are less than the dust beneath his car wheels."

"You're exaggerating," Heather said disapprovingly. She turned to Judith. "Do you happen to know when Dr. Renton is coming back?"

Judith repeated the information she had gleaned on the telephone.

"I feel really sorry for him," Laura declared, her sharp voice suddenly soft. "His brother was all the family he had."

"I shouldn't advise you to try sympathizing with him."

"Really, Heather – you might give me credit for more sense! I know perfectly well he's not the type to appreciate it."

The arrival of the doctor brought their conversation to an end, and Judith went into the surgery with him and listened while he ran through a list with Laura, making additions and deletions as they went along.

By now the waiting room was nearly full and soon Judith was ushering in the first patient. It turned out to be Mrs. Dixon, who kept the village stores. She had known the doctor's daughter since childhood, and there were greetings to be exchanged and comments to be made.

"I hear you've done ever so well at the hospital, dear. Won a medal, didn't you? My word, I expect your Dad's glad to have you home for good!"

"I suppose I should have been prepared for this," Rodney said ruefully before the next patient entered. "I can see surgery's going to take twice as long until people get used to you being here."

An hour passed quickly, but it was the individual conversations which Judith found interesting rather than the complaints. Many of these were so trivial that she wondered how her father could bring to each one the same unfailing courtesy and attention.

When they had at last finished he hurriedly drank a cup of coffee provided by Heather and then set out on his rounds. As soon as he had gone, the secretary looked rather pointedly at her watch.

"I thought having you here was supposed to speed things up."

Tempted to make a sharp reply, Judith managed to remain cool. "Everybody wanted to talk today but I expect it will soon wear off." She hesitated and added diffidently: "Before I start a session with some geriatrics Dad's fixed up for Mondays, could you spare the time to show me the filing system?"

Heather shook her head. "Sorry! I couldn't possibly stop for that now. Perhaps if you come in a bit early for evening surgery I might be able to do it then."

"Okay – I'll do that," Judith said evenly.

Why on earth had this odd antipathy sprung up between Heather and herself? Dismissing it, she turned to welcome the first of her elderly patients and, for what remained of the morning, devoted herself conscientiously to a discussion of bunions and corns, blocked ears and poor eyesight.

As she went home to get lunch, a wave of depression engulfed her. Was it for this that she had given up the daily dramas of St. Helen's Hospital, where emergencies and crises had been normal occurrences and matters of life and death had been taken in her stride?

How was she going to bear the monotony of the life she had deliberately chosen for herself? Bear it she must, or let her father down, and that she was determined never to do, even if she had to go on pretending for ever.

CHAPTER THREE

PERHAPS that particular Monday morning had been exceptionally dull, or else Judith made an unconscious mental adjustment; whatever the reason her attitude during the next few days gradually changed.

Slowly it dawned on her that there was usually at least one patient whose case held mystery, tragedy or triumph, and also that once you became aware of the background in many other cases, even the most ordinary complaint was not without interest.

Every patient was different, and the doctors were different too. Dr. Corder treated her like a child, and Dr. Graham depended on her to do some of the household shopping for him, make private phone calls in connection with his children and generally smooth his frequently thorny path.

As for Hugh Renton, she had no opportunity at first of forming an opinion of him as a doctor, for a further delay occurred and he did not return to Bedwell Green until nearly the end of the week.

It was while he was still away and his turn of duty at the surgery was being taken for him by Rodney Lidgate that drama suddenly erupted into the quiet consulting room. A white-faced but resolutely calm young teacher arrived on the heels of the last patient, leading with her a sobbing little girl who had fallen in the playground and cut the palm of her hand severely on a piece of sharp flint.

"It'll have to be stitched," the doctor said quietly as Judith began cleaning-up operations.

"Can I leave her with you?" the teacher asked anxiously. "I really ought to get back."

Scrubbing up at the sink, he glanced over his shoulder and nodded. "We'll keep her here until she's recovered from the shock, and then Judith can take her home."

There was a small cupboard-like room opening off the surgery which was used for examinations. When Mandy had been comforted and stitched up, she was installed there with a book to look at and, in a remarkably short time, was obviously fit enough to walk to her home.

"I live at No. 7 Glebe Crescent," she announced importantly. "It's one of those new bungalows down Church Lane."

With her hand in a sling, she was more than a little proud of herself and they walked along slowly, chatting in a friendly way.

It was in the midst of a long monologue from Mandy on the subject of a pet rabbit that Judith first noticed a familiar blue car which had drawn up on the corner near the church.

Surely it must be a chance resemblance ... Screwing up her eyes against the sun she tried to read the number, but it was too far away and instead she concentrated on the driver.

He had thick and longish blonde hair, of that there was no possible doubt. It *must* be – it just *had* to be Sean.

At that moment he jumped out and waved, and at the same time Mandy raised large reproachful brown eyes and said accusingly: "You aren't listening!"

"Sorry, love!" Judith jerked her gaze from Sean's approaching figure. "I am now, so please go on."

"He looks ever so funny when he washes his face – just like a pussy." She broke off again. "Who is that man?"

"A friend of mine. I think he wants to speak to me."

The totally unexpected encounter had set her pulse racing and she was annoyed because of it. Consequently her voice was cooler than she had intended when she spoke.

"Hullo, Sean – long time no see! How's your father?"

"Fine." He came nearer, his eyes on her face. "I only got back last Saturday."

"Enjoyed your holiday?"

"In a way, though it wasn't exactly a holiday." In a lower voice he added: "The ward doesn't seem the same without you. I can't seem to realise that you aren't just off duty, that you'll *never* be on duty there again."

"I've got quite used to the idea myself," Judith said airily.

Sean's gaze dropped to where Mandy stood impatiently waiting. "Where are you going with the child?"

"Nurse is taking me home," she informed him before Judith could speak. "I had a nasty fall in the playground and cut my hand." With her unbandaged hand she tugged at Judith's arm. "Come on – I want to tell my mummy about it."

"I've got to go on duty at two o'clock," Sean said. "I thought you'd be free when surgery was over."

"Oh no, I've got patients of my now to see when

I've delivered Mandy," replied Judith. "Why didn't you ring up to find out when I finished?"

There was impatience in her tone and he stared at her in slight bewilderment, taken aback at the lack of welcome. Not being psychic, he had no means of knowing what she was really asking him was: "Why did you disappear like that? Why didn't you write or phone while you were away?"

"I didn't think of it, I suppose," he said lamely.

He looked so disappointed that Judith softened. "If you could bear to hang around in Bedwell Green for an hour or so, we could meet when I come off duty. I don't expect to be late today."

Sean's face instantly brightened. "Okay, I'll do that, and in the meantime can I drive you to wherever you're going?"

Mandy's impatience was by now reaching explosion point and so they both got into the small shabby car and were driven down Church Lane.

Almost at once they passed the church standing quietly among its lichen-covered tombs and surrounded by tall elms. The double-fronted house nearly opposite was Birch Cottage. It stood in a small garden in which roses, sweet peas and honeysuckle did battle with the weeds and only triumphed because of their greater height. Mrs. Crowfield was obviously not much of a gardener, or else she didn't have the time to give to it.

"Not far now," Mandy said, as they rapidly approached the entrance to Glebe Crescent.

When the child had been handed over and her mother's alarm soothed, Judith returned to Sean's car.

"Why don't you come and have lunch with us?"

she suggested impulsively. "You'd still have plenty of time to get back by two o'clock and you've got to eat somewhere in any case."

"Super idea!" His ingenuous expression gave her no hint that he had been hoping for just such an invitation. "Hop in, and let's get you back to the surgery so you can get finished as soon as possible."

As she weighed babies and gave advice on childish ailments, Judith almost forgot all about him, but it was pleasing to come out later on and find him waiting for her, and to know that she could spend an hour or so enjoying hospital gossip.

Installed in the kitchen at Grove Farm House, Sean watched her scraping new potatoes with interest.

"Seems kinda funny you turning out so domesticated," he commented.

"Anybody can be domesticated if they have to."

"Not always successfully, I should have thought."

"How do you whether I'm successful?" She turned round, laughing. "You'd better wait until you've had lunch before you make statements like that."

But the meal was such a simple one – cold meat and salad followed by fresh fruit – that Sean was able to assure his hostess that he had enjoyed it thoroughly. They had eaten by themselves, since Dr. Lidgate had been delayed, and the tête-à-tête meal seemed to have completely restored their old friendly relationship.

Consequently, when the time came for him to leave for Cumberton, it seemed quite natural for him to kiss Judith goodbye and to announce that he would be coming over again as soon as he could.

"I can't promise to be free," she protested.

"I'll ring first next time. I suppose it was a bit daft not to do so today, but it turned out okay in the end." He smiled, waved his hand and drove away with a noisy crunch of tyres on the gravel.

Judith watched him go with mixed feelings. Now that he was no longer with her, she couldn't imagine why she had weakened and let him come back into her life after a silence of at least three weeks. In any case, she hadn't really intended to keep up with him when she left the hospital, so what in the world did she think she was doing?

Finding no satisfactory answer, she went to re-lay the table for her father's lunch.

He came in soon afterwards, looking hot and tired. "I'll be glad when Hugh gets back," he said, sitting down with a sigh.

"But doesn't Dr. Corder go on holiday next week? That means you're still one short."

"There's a lot of difference between doing without John and not having Hugh working in the practice, as you'll find out before long." Rodney paused to help himself liberally to salad. "It's about time we heard from him again – Hugh, I mean – he promised he'd ring up and let us know when to expect him."

"You'll probably get a call from him this evening," Judith said soothingly.

She was right about that, but her father was out when the young doctor telephoned and she took a message for him.

"Tell him I'll be back tomorrow afternoon," Hugh announced. "I'm not sure what time, but I don't suppose he'll want me to make any calls until the morning."

He broke off but Judith sensed that he was about to add something. After making an appropriate reply she waited for a moment but Hugh must have changed his mind for he merely said: "Well, that's all then, thanks," and rang off.

He didn't believe in wasting time on the telephone, she reflected as she replaced her own receiver and scribbled a note on the pad.

She would have been considerably surprised if she had known of the length of his conversation with his landlady.

Mrs. Crowfield received her own call that same evening. After giving her the information concerning his return, Hugh plunged straight into the subject which he had been on the brink of mentioning to Judith.

"By the way, I'm not coming back alone, Mrs. Crowfield. I shall have my niece with me. I know you've got a couple of spare rooms, so I hope you won't mind letting her have one of them."

"A child!" There was dismay in Elizabeth Crowfield's voice. "Who's to look after her, doctor?"

"Melanie's not a child – she's perfectly capable of looking after herself."

"How old is she then?" she asked suspiciously.

"Just coming up to fifteen, and quite grown up for her age. I'm sure she won't be any trouble."

Privately, Mrs. Crowfield found herself unable to share his confidence, but she remembered what a terrible tragedy had overtaken the poor girl and scarcely liked to refuse to have her.

"How long do you want her to stay?" she asked bluntly.

There was a brief pause and then Hugh said, with

considerably less than his usual briskness: "It's hard to say. It depends so much on how things go. Unfortunately Melanie doesn't get on with her maternal grandparents and they're both in rather poor health, to say nothing of being absolutely shattered – by what has happened. The poor kid hasn't anywhere else to go."

"That seems to settle it then," Mrs. Crowfield said bleakly.

"Thank you – I'm very grateful. Er – actually there is another good reason for me to keep an eye on her. My brother appointed me her guardian in his will."

"It's a good thing you've got a place where you *can* take her; otherwise you might find it rather awkward."

Over the wires she could feel that Hugh had no idea of her real meaning and she did not enlarge on it further. He would find out in time perhaps.

"We'll be arriving on Friday afternoon." The businesslike tone was back again. "I don't suppose you'll be back from Cumberton but it doesn't matter. In the meantime, will you please work out how much extra you'd like me to pay?"

So that was that. Mrs. Crowfield left the telephone with a sense of deep foreboding. She had never really wanted to take a lodger in the first place but the money was useful and enabled her to have expensive holidays she couldn't otherwise have afforded, and also to pay for help with the housework.

And it had worked out very well. Hugh Renton was unobtrusive – on the whole – and courteous, and out a great deal. In fact, the only fault she had so far found with him was that he took no interest in the garden and had never offered to help. And that, she freely admitted to herself, would be more than any landlady had a right to expect.

But now he had blotted his copybook well and truly. Just coming up to fifteen, he'd said, which meant that Melanie was at just about the most difficult period of her teens, neither child nor adult. As a teacher in a girls' school, Elizabeth was well aware of the problems which might arise.

With some idea of getting the unwholesome task over quickly, she went upstairs and debated which of her two rooms should be given to the stranger. The house was divided into two equal parts, with a bathroom built out at the back. At present Hugh occupied the front bedroom on one side and she slept in the corresponding room on the other side. The obvious thing to do was to give Melanie the room next to her uncle, thus keeping the width of the landing between herself and her unwelcome lodger.

What would the girl do when Hugh had to work all the evening, for goodness' sake?

Shelving the problem, which wasn't really one of hers – though she had a horrible feeling that it might become so – Elizabeth prepared the room as quickly as possible and went downstairs to consider the question of food.

When she returned at the end of afternoon school the following day, Hugh's car was outside Birch Cottage and there were voices coming from his sitting room.

He had evidently heard her car stop and he came out at once to meet her. Hovering behind him was a tall, very slender girl with pale gold hair falling nearly to her waist and a thin face in which the vivid blue eyes appeared sunken and haunted.

Elizabeth had never possessed a motherly heart, but she was touched nevertheless. She held out her hand and took the girl's limp one in a warm clasp.

"Hullo, Melanie! I expect you're tired and hungry after your journey. I'll get busy in the kitchen and hurry up the evening meal."

"I'm not hungry." The girl's voice matched her listless handshake. "I've hardly eaten anything all the week, have I, Hugh?"

"You'll soon get your appetite back in the fresh country air," he told her, speaking with a heartiness quite foreign to him.

His landlady left them on their own and continued on her way to the kitchen. Not quite fifteen, indeed! Well, no one would find that easy to believe. Her long slim legs in faded jeans could easily have belonged to an eighteen-year-old, and her looks in general had nothing young about them, though that might be due to her shocking experience.

At present Elizabeth hardly knew what to make of the newcomer, and she was no nearer forming an opinion by the end of the evening. As she followed her usual custom of laying the table for breakfast overnight, she thought with some amusement that it might be interesting to discover what the reaction of the village turned out to be.

At Grove Farm House they heard the news from Hugh himself. He called late that evening to ask after his patients and at the end of an entirely professional conversation, suddenly announced nonchalantly: "I brought my niece back with me. It seemed the only thing to do."

"Good idea!" Rodney said cheerfully after a startled pause. "It's splendid for the child to get right away. Er – she wasn't with her parents, I take it?"

"She was at her boarding school, but I couldn't leave her there. She was much too upset."

Hugh frowned, remembering how Melanie had clung to him sobbing and how desperately sorry for her he had felt.

"Yes, yes, of course. I'm sure you did the right thing but – " Rodney hesitated and then added delicately: "No doubt Mrs. Crowfield will entirely understand the situation and sympathise."

"Oh yes – she's been helpfulness itself," Hugh assured him innocently.

There was a pause and then Judith put in: "Won't your niece be very lonely while you're working? Is she old enough to be left on her own for so long?"

"She's certainly old enough." Why, just because he was in his twenties, did people assume that his brother had been about the same age? Ten years had separated them and David had been getting on for forty when he died.

"Well, that's a help anyway," Rodney said.

Hugh's eyes switched to Judith. "I was wondering – " He broke off abruptly, but it was easy for her to guess what he had been going to say.

A strange instinctive reluctance tried to restrain her from offering assistance. It wouldn't do, she found herself arguing internally, to get too involved with a child just now, no matter how much she liked children. They were always demanding, and a little girl who had lost both parents was likely to be particularly so. It would be no kindness to offer friendship and then find that the newcomer was taking up time she couldn't spare.

And yet – how could she possibly withhold an offer of help under such tragic circumstances?

Both men were now looking at her and Judith found herself following the dictates of her heart without further hesitation.

"Perhaps she would like to come round here sometimes? I finish at the surgery about half-past ten and I could call for her and bring her back with me after I've held my clinic. Or perhaps the afternoon would be better – I've got more time then – "

For the first time during their brief acquaintance she saw Hugh's smile.

"That's very good of you, Judith, and it takes a weight off my mind. I'll tell Melanie she can come round and see you whenever she likes. There's no need for you to bother to call for her."

It wasn't exactly what she had offered, but Judith let it pass. After all, it couldn't be for long because Melanie would have to return to school when she was feeling a bit better.

Ignoring the fact that it would soon be the end of the summer term, Judith went off to make coffee.

The next day she half expected to find a small forlorn girl on her doorstep every time the bell rang, but Melanie made no move and it was not until the fourth day, when Hugh happened to be taking evening surgery, that the subject was again raised.

"I've seen nothing of your niece," Judith remarked when she had closed the door on the last patient. "I was wondering if she was too shy to come round on her own."

"I think she's been too apathetic," Hugh told her, looking worried. "She seems to be spending most of her time reading at present."

"Do you think it would be a good idea for me to come and collect her, as I at first suggested?"

He pushed back the lock of hair which had fallen over his forehead and gave the question his serious consideration.

"Personally I think it would be better if Melanie made the effort to get to Grove Farm House. I'll remind her about it at lunchtime and she'll probably turn up before long." A look of embarrasment crossed his face. "She seems to have rather a pathetic wish to please me at the moment."

"I'll hope to see her soon then." Judith dismissed the subject and began to tidy the surgery while the doctor looked through the list of his evening calls.

Whatever he said to Melanie was evidently effective. The following afternoon Judith was in the kitchen topping and tailing gooseberries when the telephone rang. A youthful, rather high voice said hesitatingly: "Is that Judith? It's Melanie here. Hugh says I ought to go and see you but I'm not sure *exactly* where you live."

"Grove Farm House," answered Judith. "It's easy to find because it overlooks the Green, on the opposite side from the surgery. Are you coming round now?"

"I thought I would. Actually, I was wondering if you've got anything to read?"

"Oh yes, I'm sure I can find you some books." There was in her own bedroom a whole shelf of books she had enjoyed during her own schooldays. "You'd better come and have a look."

"Okay." There was a click and the line went dead.

As she went upstairs to check that her room was reasonably tidy, Judith reflected how fortunate it was that Melanie was so fond of reading. At least she wouldn't expect people to play games with her.

She picked out a few books which were among her own favourites and laid them ready on the bed. And almost immediately the front door bell rang.

CHAPTER FOUR

As SHE opened the door Judith was aware of the sound of pop music and she looked in astonishment at the tall girl – taller than herself – who stood in the porch, a transistor set in her hand.

Perhaps she had brought a message for the doctor – she couldn't possibly be Hugh Renton's niece. But as soon as the girl spoke she knew that it really was Melanie.

"Hullo! You said I could come round and choose some books." The voice was casual – almost rudely so – but there was an undercurrent of nervousness.

"Yes, of course. Do come in!" Judith flung the door wide in an effort to make up for her apparent lack of welcome.

"I brought my tranny so I could listen to it on the way." Melanie put the small set to her ear and hummed a few notes, breaking off to say sharply: "Why do you keep staring at me?"

"I didn't realise I was." Judith hastily averted her eyes from the pale face with its oriental make-up round the eyes and strange lack of youthfulness. "The thing is, I was expecting someone much younger. Your uncle didn't tell us you were so – so grown up."

"I'm nearly fifteen. I expect you thought I'd turn out to be a little girl!"

"Well, yes, I did rather. I'm afraid the books I looked out for you won't do at all."

"I hoped you'd have some paperbacks," Melanie

said, pausing in the hall and swaying slightly to the rhythm of the music which she evidently did not intend to switch off. "I like the American crime writers best, but they don't have any in the village shop, and I can't afford to keep buying them anyway."

"I think I can find a few. Come and have a look." As they went upstairs, Judith added: "Are you *sure* you're under fifteen? You look much more than that."

"It's because I'm tall and, of course, it's natural I should look older after – after what's just happened. It was a terribly *ageing* experience."

"Yes, I'm sure it was. We were all most dreadfully sorry when we heard about it."

Judith opened her bedroom door and hurried gathered up the schoolgirlish literature spread out on the bed, indicating a shelf of paperbacks instead. "Have a look through those and take anything you like. I'll be in the kitchen when you're ready to come down."

Returning to the topping and tailing of the gooseberries, she gradually recovered from her surprise, reflecting that it would, in a way, be easier to cope with the sophisticated teenager who had come into her life than with the more childish version she had been expecting. The girl seemed to get on well with older people, since she had apparently established a good relationship with her uncle, and it might be possible to get really friendly with her.

Melanie stayed all the afternoon, spending most of her time lying on the lawn with the "tranny" close to her head and a book held up before her eyes. She was no trouble at all and Judith found little difficulty in pressing her warmly to come whenever she felt like it.

"There's a library van which comes to the village once a fortnight," she added. "I expect you could get some books from it when you've exhausted the supply of paperbacks."

"Okay – er – thanks." With a limp wave of her hand, Melanie drifted away.

After that she came to Grove Farm House quite frequently, continuing to be quiet and detached. If it had not been for the faint murmur of pop music, Judith would sometimes hardly have realised she was there.

Nevertheless, she felt a vague sense of dissatisfaction. She had honestly meant to be helpful, perhaps even play the role of an older sister to Melanie, and she was getting nowhere at all with the girl. She knew her no better at the end of her sixth visit than she had done at the beginning.

"I suppose you'll be going back to school soon?" she ventured to ask one day.

For the first time Melanie showed strong feeling. "No, I'm not! Hugh said I needn't if I didn't want to, not this term anyway. I couldn't bear it – honestly I couldn't! The girls in my form are all so *young* and *boring* – I just couldn't stand being with them again after all I've been through."

"But don't you find it rather boring living in Bedwell Green without anybody your own age to be friendly with?"

Melanie shook her head vigorously, her long hair swinging round her face. "I'm never bored with Hugh – I feels he *understands* me perfectly. And when he's not there, well – I manage." A faint smile made her look suddenly attractive. "I can always come round here, Judy, and I like sitting in your garden and reading with you busy in the house."

Judith was so astonished at such an expression of appreciation that she almost gasped. This was a real step forward, and when Hugh himself added a word of thanks she felt that her efforts had been well rewarded.

"I really am grateful to you for helping out with Melanie, Judith. It's been a weight off my mind knowing she had you to turn to. Mrs. Crowfield's been very good but she's a bit of a schoolmarm sometimes and my niece is old enough not to care much for that sort of thing."

"I shouldn't imagine she'd fancy being bossed around much," Judith glanced down at him where he sat at the desk in the surgery. "Except by you, of course. Did you know that you've become the sun and moon and stars to her?"

"Don't be ridicuous!" He had flushed with angry embarrassment. "It's natural she should be a bit clinging under the circumstances. After she's returned to school, she won't give me another thought."

"Which won't be until the autumn term, I gather?"

"I didn't want to force her just now, and the headmistress said it wouldn't be worthwhile returning this term, unless Melanie herself wanted to. I think she needs a period of peace and quiet in which to start the natural processes of healing."

It all sounded very reasonable and Judith felt sure he was right; nevertheless, she was aware of a slight feeling of disquiet which was not assuaged by one or two conversations she had with patients.

"Only fourteen, did you say?" Mrs. Bradbury, who was crippled with arthritis and never went anywhere except to the surgery, was always up-to-date with events in the village. "To my mind, Nurse, she could easily be three years older."

"She isn't really, I assure you." Judith began the difficult process of hoisting the old lady on to her feet.

"Well, of course, you can't tell with girls these days and it isn't their real age that matters so much as the way they look and behave. That Melanie Renton looks as though she'd be ripe for having a boyfriend. Sexy, that's what she is."

"Mrs. Bradbury – you're not to talk like that about her! She's a very nice, quiet girl – "

"Ah!" said the patient darkly. "They're always the worst. Still waters run deep, don't they say? Ouch, Nurse – don't go so quick! I'm stiffer than ever this morning and I reckon that means there's a change in the weather coming."

And at the village shop, Mrs. Dixon said: "How much longer is that niece of Dr. Renton's going to be here, Judith? It's not a healthy life for a young girl being on her own so much. I know you do your best for her but she needs friends of her own age."

"Her uncle thinks it's good for her to live quietly just now."

"He could be wrong, you know. All that reading doesn't seem natural to me; she'd be better off playing tennis and having fun with her friends."

"She's just suffered a terrible loss," Judith protested indignantly.

"Yes, of course, poor child." Mrs. Dixon looked slightly ashamed of her criticism. "It'll all work out all right, I expect, and it's none of our business after all. Two pounds of tomatoes, did you say? And how about a nice lettuce? I've got some lovely ones only cut this morning."

Judith left the shop with her arms full and began to hurry home. It was her father's day off and she hoped that he might actually eat lunch on time.

Just as she started to cross the Green a car pulled up on the road nearby and the passenger wound the window down.

"Judy! Stop a minute – "

Judith swung round and found the object of her conversation with Mrs. Dixon looking out at her with quite an animated expression on her face.

"I probably won't be coming round this afternoon," Melanie called. "Hugh's got to visit a patient who's staying at Duneham and he's taking me with him. We're going to have lunch out and I don't know when we'll be back."

"It's old Dr. Jameson," Hugh explained, seeing Judith's surprise. "He's on holiday and he seems to have picked up some sort of tummy bug. I know it sounds very like preferential treatment but it's only thirty miles from here and he is rather a special case. Didn't he start this practice about fifty years ago?"

"That's right, and he still lives in the district, but he's so normally healthy that I don't suppose you've met him." She hesitated. "Are you sure you can spare the time to go? I don't suppose Dad would mind – "

"I'm not going to spoil his day off," Hugh said emphatically. "He had to do a lot of my work while I was away."

Judith did not argue though she felt sure her father would not have objected at all, and she herself would have enjoyed a trip to the seaside. Telling herself that Melanie needed the outing far more than she did, she waved goodbye and walked on across the Green.

"She's nice, isn't she?" Melanie said, watching her thoughtfully. "I wouldn't call her exactly an *interesting* person but she's kind and doesn't make a fuss about things which don't matter."

"Like what?" Hugh asked curiously.

"Well, she leaves me alone, instead of always trying to make me *do* things. Why should I do anything if I don't want to?"

"Why indeed!"

"Now you're laughing at me," she reproached him.

"No, I'm not." He patted her bare arm in what he believed to be an avuncular way. "I was only thinking that most people have to do a great many things they don't want to. *I* certainly do."

They had turned a corner and come face to face with a flock of sheep. The woolly baa-ing creatures poured past on both sides of the car in a frenzy of anxiety and Hugh was obliged to halt until they were all clear.

Consequently he did not at first notice that his niece had suddenly dissolved into tears.

"I suppose that means you don't want me staying with you," Melanie drew a long quivering breath. "And I do try so hard not to be a nuisance. I've absolutely *longed* to go with you on your rounds but I've never said a word about it and this is the first time you've ever taken me."

"My dear girl – !" Hugh, who had had his foot on the accelerator, removed it hastily and applied the brake. "You're talking absolute nonsense. Of course I want to have you with me – we've both been through a shattering experience – though it was worse for you, naturally, and I think we can help each other to get back on an even keel."

As Melanie continued to sob, he put his hand over hers and squeezed it. "Do stop crying, love. I don't like seeing you so upset. You'll have me joining in if you don't watch it, and what on earth would we look like, sitting here in the car and bawling our heads off?"

The suggestion produced, as he had hoped it would, an outburst of hysterical laughter.

"Men don't cry," Melanie said when she had recovered a little.

"They're not supposed to, poor blighters, but that doesn't mean they never feel like it."

"I didn't know that." She paused to think it over and then reverted to the second accusation. "If you like having me with you, why have you never invited me to go out with you on your rounds?"

It had never entered his head to do so, but he did not think it would be politic to put it so bluntly.

"For several reasons, Melanie. I think you'd be bored after a while, just sitting in the car, and no doctor ever knows what time he will get back from a busy round, so it could be quite a long wait with nothing to do."

"I could read and listen to my tranny."

"You'd be far better off reading in a more comfortable place, and – quite frankly – I don't think I could stand the transistor."

"Oh!" Once more she was silent and then she said reproachfully: "That's only one reason."

He could not possibly tell her that he didn't want her company when he was working, fond as he was of her, that he preferred to think only of his patients, and so he just said lightly: "I don't want you to lose the use of your legs! To my way of thinking, you do too much lolling about as it is."

"What would I do instead?" she demanded.

Hugh laughed. "You've got me there! I haven't the faintest idea, so let's drop the subject, shall we?"

He speeded up and was soon negotiating a busy roundabout where they joined the dual carriageway which would take them to the popular seaside resort of Duneham.

Lunch was a pleasant meal, not marred either by argument or tragic thoughts, and then Melanie went to walk along the promenade while Hugh called on Dr. Jameson, who was not entirely pleased at being attended by a young man instead of one of the older partners.

Fortunately Hugh's professional manner and obvious competence soothed him and they parted amicably.

Melanie was very silent on the homeward journey, but as soon as they reached Bedwell Green she said with a long sigh: "I did enjoy that so much, Hugh. Will Dr. Jameson need another visit?"

"Only if the prescription I left with him doesn't work, and it jolly well ought to." He smiled down at her. "I can't spare the time to make many long trips like this."

"No, I suppose not," she said despondently. "I don't think you ought to take me back to Birch

Cottage as you're so late with your afternoon calls. I could stay in the car just this once, couldn't I?" Hopefully, she glanced up at him from beneath her lashes.

"Sorry, love, but it's just not on. How about visiting Judith instead of going home?"

"I told her I wasn't coming today, and I don't suppose she'll want me as her father is at home."

"Please yourself," Hugh said in a carefully casual tone and turned down Church Lane.

Melanie got out in a very aggrieved frame of mind, but by the time he returned – three hours later – she had repented of her bad mood and greeted him – considerably to his embarrassment – by rushing out to fling herself into his arms as soon as he stepped out of the car.

"I'm sorry I was so cross, Hugh! I didn't mean it – really I didn't. I think you're absolutely right not to let yourself be distracted by me when you're visiting patients, and I won't ever try to persuade you to take me round with you again."

He bent his head and dropped an impulsive kiss on her silky hair, glad that she was now prepared to be sensible but also wishing that she wouldn't be so dramatic about it.

He did not notice that a gnarled hand was holding back the curtain in the front room of a cottage a little further down the road, and that Mrs. Bradbury had witnessed the affectionate greeting. Even if he had, he would probably not have considered it of any importance.

Judith heard about it the next morning.

"Kissing him she was, Nurse, and him kissing her back. I know they're related and all that but it doesn't seem right to me, not with him being such a young man and the girl so old-looking for her age."

"You've got a thoroughly nasty mind, Mrs. Bradbury," Judith said severely, knowing that she would not give offence.

"It's not me, Nurse – it's them others. Proper lot of gossips they are in Bedwell Green. You'd be surprised!"

"I don't suppose I would, but there's really no need for anybody to hear about Melanie very naturally rushing out to greet her uncle. You don't *have* to talk about it."

"I shouldn't dream of telling anybody," said the old lady indignantly. "Except you, of course, and that's different, you being in the medical profession and having sealed lips."

Nevertheless, by the end of the day nearly everybody in Bedwell Green – except the commuters, who could not have cared less – knew about the incident.

Mrs. Bradbury had been quite right, Judith reflected, when she blamed the doctor's youth and Melanie's maturity for the general attitude towards them both. It was ridiculous really – why on earth shouldn't Hugh kiss his niece? – and no doubt few people thought any the worse of them for their affection towards each other, but somehow people just didn't seem able to refrain from commenting on it.

Very probably it was because of the blaze of publicity in which a doctor living in a small community was obliged to exist, and there was nothing any of the four doctors could do about that, except try to be extra careful.

The conclusion reminded her uncomfortably of

another matter which would give the village opportunity for conjecture if it ever became generally known.

The previous afternoon she had been helping her father in the garden when he suddenly straightened up and looked at her.

"I was just wondering if you'd be going into Cumberton soon, Judy. I don't think you've been near the place since you came home."

"I haven't needed to," she answered. "Mrs. Dixon keeps a wonderful stock at her shop."

"I wasn't thinking so much of household shopping, but I should have thought you'd want to go just for a change and to buy things for yourself – tights and all that."

Judith bent over an obstinate weed and pulled so hard that it broke off, leaving its roots in the ground. She had deliberately stayed away from the town because she wasn't sure what effect the sight of the hospital would have on her. And in Cumberton you couldn't avoid seeing St. Helen's; it stood on a slight hill and dominated the town.

"Mrs. Dixon sells tights and I haven't needed anything else. Why do you ask?"

It was the opening Rodney had been hoping for and he gladly plunged in at once.

"I'd be grateful if you'd undertake a commission for me. I happen to know it's Heather's birthday next week and I want to give her a really nice present as a token of gratitude for all the extra work she did before you came home."

Judith abandoned the weed and stared at him in astonishment. "Didn't you pay her for the additional hours? I took it for granted you would."

"I tried to at first." Rodney avoided her gaze and leaned on his hoe, staring at the ground. "She wouldn't hear of it and I felt I'd insulted her. She's a very generous person, you know, and likes doing things for people."

Judith was silent for a moment. She was prejudiced against Heather – she admitted it freely in the privacy of her thoughts – and therefore unable to judge her fairly.

"So what do you want me to get?" she asked eventually.

"My dear girl, I haven't the faintest idea! I thought you'd come up with some suggestions."

"How about a piece of good costume jewellery?"

"Sounds a splemdid idea," Rodney said with relief. "I'll leave it to you to choose something suitable, but get it done soon because there isn't much time left."

"I could catch the two o'clock bus tomorrow if you like, but it will make me a little bit late for evening surgery."

"Doesn't matter. I'm taking it anyway, and I shall understand the reason." He glanced across at her. "When you've done your shopping, why don't you look up some of your friends?"

"Maybe I will."

But her friends all worked at St. Helen's and she wasn't at all sure whether she wanted to look them up. Or – on the other hand – whether she would be able to keep away.

CHAPTER FIVE

ANXIOUS to get her commission satisfactorily dealt with as soon as possible, Judith went straight from the bus station to the jewellers' at the corner of Market Street.

She had decided on a pendant and found the choice almost bewildering. Eventually she selected what seemed to her to be the most attractive – an intricate metal design set with green stones – and she purchased it, hoping that it would please both her father and the recipient. Heather, she decided after some thought, had greenish eyes, so the pendant should suit her very well.

Outside the shop she paused and debated what to do next. It was more than two hours before the return bus; she could potter round the shops and perhaps buy a new dress, she might even see a film, or she could visit St. Helen's and see if any of her friends were off duty.

It was no problem at all really. Within seconds Judith was walking briskly away from Market Street, towards the hospital.

Stella's flat was on the way and she stopped there first, but her ring at the bell was unanswered. Her next call was at the staff nurses' flatlets where she hoped by studying the "in" and "out" board to find someone she knew well enough to call on unexpectedly.

There was no need to look at the board. As she

entered the small vestibule she heard her name called and swung round to find Stella herself following her in.

She was looking very smart in the saxe-blue dress of a staff nurse and Judith's pleasure at seeing her was pierced by a stab of envy.

"What are you doing here?" she asked in surprise when they had greeted each other.

"I've given up the other flat. My sister decided to get married and to live at home for a while so as to save as much money as possible. I didn't want to share with anyone else and these staff nurses' flats are really very nice."

"Somehow I'd forgotten you'd be a staff nurse now," Judith said slowly.

"You'd have been one too if you'd stayed on," Stella looked at her searchingly. "How's it working out, Judy? Do you like living in a village again and – all the rest of it?"

"I've settled down now." Her tone was evasive and Stella did not press her further.

"Come up to my flat and have a cuppa. I'm off duty until five o'clock."

As they emerged from the lift and Stella fitted her key into the lock, Judith was again conscious of the sharpness of envy. The flat was only small but it was a place of one's own, a refuge and a background, somewhere in which to be alone or entertain according to the need of the moment.

She must be out of her mind! She had a whole *house* where she could do more or less what she liked, and a large bedroom which was entirely her own, to say nothing of beautiful country surroundings instead of a view of roofs and chimney pots.

"How's Sean?" she asked abruptly when they had settled themselves comfortably in armchairs.

"Missing you, I think," answered Stella.

"You have to be joking! Sean's not the sort to miss people enough for it to show."

"I wouldn't have thought so either, but he's certainly quieter than he used to be."

"Could be he's worried about his father."

"I thought he was okay now. It seems to have been a very mild seizure." Stella jumped up again as the electric kettle began to boil over. "Don't you want Sean to miss you?"

"You know I don't! I intended to make a clean break when I left St. Helen's but – well, he turned up at Bedwell Green one day and we more or less picked things up where we left off. I haven't seen him since though."

"I can't think why you have to bother so much about it, Judy." Stella reappeared in the doorway which led to the tiny kitchen. "Why don't you just accept what comes and stop analysing people and worrying over them? You're not seriously in love with Sean, so what's it matter if you go on seeing him? It can't be for long because he'll be off to a different job in a few months."

Judith did not answer immediately, and then she said in a low voice: "Perhaps I'm afraid I might get serious about him, and that would upset all my plans for looking after Dad."

"You don't mean to devote the rest of your life to your father, surely!" Stella exclaimed in astonishment.

"I haven't looked that far ahead."

"I should hope not! I've got no use at all for self-sacrificing daughters and selfish grasping parents who batten on them, and I wouldn't like to think a friend of mine was such a fool." She tossed her head back defiantly, obviously expecting an indignant outburst, but Judith only laughed.

"There's no need to get so worked up. I'm still only twenty-one and I've not been living at home more than a few weeks." Her tone was suddenly serious. "And you're not to feel sorry for me! I *like* what I'm doing and I find the village patients very interesting, and now that I'm getting used to it I even like running the house."

Stella smiled and began to pour out the tea, and after that they talked about less controversial matters, the nurses in their set who had remained at the hospital, the sudden engagement of one of the sisters to a widowed consultant, and the amazing and miraculous recovery of a patient whose case had been regarded as utterly hopeless.

Judith could have gone on sitting there indefinitely while Stella was willing and able to keep up her share of the conversation, but inevitably the time grew near for her return to duty.

"I'll walk over to the hospital with you," Judith said. "My bus isn't due for another half-hour."

As they crossed the grounds the familiar antiseptic smell filtered out to greet her, mingling with the sweet smell of the roses beside the path so that in her imagination she was once more back on the ward, arranging the flowers or working hard beside the doctors to save a life, or doing any of the dozens of jobs in between these extremes.

"I won't come any further." She halted abruptly

outside the swing doors. "I don't want to lose my bus."

"Okay." Stella had understood the real reason and made no attempt to argue. "See you some time!"

She vanished into a side entrance and Judith turned away. As she did so there came the sound of hurrying footsteps snd a voice calling, a well-known voice which caused her to turn with the same quickening of the pulses which she had experienced when Sean appeared suddenly in the village.

He arrived at a gallop, his white coat flapping open and the stethoscope swinging.

"Why didn't you tell me you were coming?" he demanded.

"I didn't know myself." Judith avoided adding that she wouldn't have told him anyway. "I was in Cumberton and I thought I'd see if Stella was free. We've spent most of the afternoon together and now I'm off to catch my bus."

"I'll drive you," Sean said at once. "I can get away for an hour."

"Please don't bother – "

He came closer and looked into her eyes. "You know it isn't a bother, Judy, so why pretend? I'm glad to have the chance of a short time with you."

His unusual seriousness made her uneasy, but her own pleasure at seeing him triumphed and she agreed to the lift without further argument.

"I'm sorry I haven't managed to get over to Bedwell Green again," Sean said as they swept down the drive. "You know what it's like being a house-man at a busy hospital – I don't get a lot of time off even now, though it's much better than it used to be."

He paused to look left and right before emerging on to the road. "And we've had a run of emergency operations lately too. I like to attend as many of those as I can manage."

"You don't have to do all this explaining," Judith pointed out.

"I was afraid I didn't! You couldn't care less whether I come over or not, could you?"

Hoping that it was a rhetorical question, she made no reply and thereafter Sean concentrated on negotiating the rush hour traffic. But when they were on the road to Bedwell Green he began talking again.

"I was going to phone you this week, as a matter of fact. There's a dance on at the hospital on the fourteenth and I wanted to ask if you could come."

"There's a dance every Friday night," Judith said quickly.

"Yeah, but this one is special, with a live band. It's to raise money towards installing squash courts."

"I don't think I could get very excited about that." She was still playing for time. "Isn't squash a game played almost entirely by men?"

"You're out of date, love. Quite a lot of girls are getting interested. So how about it?"

Judith hesitated, part of her longing to accept the invitation, and not only because it would be Sean who had issued it but also because it would be a wonderful opportunity to mingle with the well-known hospital personalities and pretend that she still belonged.

But the fact remained that she was getting more and more involved with Sean and she hadn't intended to. And then Stella's comment flashed into her mind. Perhaps she *was* being ridiculous to take it all so seriously. Wouldn't it be much more sensible just to say that she'd like to go to the dance, and leave it at that?

"I don't find all this doubtfulness of yours very flattering," Sean was saying ruefully.

"I'm sorry!" She turned towards him and laughed. "I'd love to come, and thanks for asking me. It's Friday week, isn't it? What time do you want me to be ready?"

They made their arrangements and drove on more happily. When they reached Grove House Farm Judith apologised for not inviting him in, saying that she was already late for evening surgery.

"I couldn't spare the time anyway." He looked up at her where she stood by the open window, and the expression in his eyes caused her to veil her own hastily. "Cheerio for now, Judy."

Judith put the pendant in a safe place and changed quickly into uniform. As she crossed the Green she felt glad that her father would understand the reason for her non-appearance at the proper time. Not that she was more than a few minutes late, for the lift with Sean had brought her home much quicker than the bus would have done.

Heather, of course, did not approve of *any* lateness. She was putting the cover on her typewriter when Judith whisked past and she looked rather pointedly at her watch.

"The first patient has already gone in."

"Did you look up the notes for me? Thanks very much!" With a bright smile which faded almost instantly, Judith vanished into the surgery.

Why on earth couldn't she like Heather when her father obviously thought so highly of her? She was a wonderful worker, entirely loyal and trustworthy, and she had the advantage of knowing the practice from A to Z. And yet . . .

With an effort Judith brought her attention sharply back to her duties and went to help her father with a nervous child who was objecting strenuously to having a blood sample taken, and whose mother was announcing loudly that she "couldn't bear to look".

Later on, when the patients had all been dealt with and Heather had long since departed, Rodney said eagerly: "Did you get something nice?"

"I think so." Judith described the pendant. "I put it in the small drawer of your desk in the study. When actually is Heather's birthday?"

"Wednesday." He turned the pages of a diary. "I'm not on morning surgery duty that day, so you'll have to give it to her when you come over."

"I expect she'd rather have it direct from you. Why don't you try and fit in a special visit? She'd appreciate that."

She was trying hard to make up for the lack of enthusiasm in her own mind, about which he knew nothing, and was pleased because she seemed to have said just the right thing.

"Good idea, Judy! I'll do that."

When Wednesday came, she even managed to say brightly: "Happy birthday, Heather!" on her arrival at the surgery.

The secretary looked astonished. "How on earth did you know?"

"My father told me."

"Oh, I see." Heather flushed slightly and then sighed. "I don't go much for birthdays nowadays,

I'm afraid. Once you get over thirty, they lose a lot of their charm."

How old was she? Judith wondered. Thirty-five? Perhaps nearly forty. With unmarried women who had led uneventful lives it was often hard to tell.

Surgery that morning was taken by Dr. Corder, a distinguished-looking man with thinning grey hair and a small greyish-white moustache. Not approving of Judith's presence, he ignored her as much as possible, except when something needed fetching, but she was used to this treatment by now and did not let it trouble her.

About halfway through surgery hour, she went into the office to look up some information and was surprised to find the secretary with her head bent over her desk. There was a small familiar package open in front of her and for one awful moment Judith thought she was crying.

The closing of the door caused Heather to jerk her head up hastily, and Judith said at once: "Do you like it?"

"Oh yes – it's beautiful! And such a surprise." She picked up the pretty trinket. "Your father has wonderful taste."

She must think he'd chosen it himself. Anxious not to disillusion her, Judith agreed that he had. "Put it on and let me see how you look in it."

"I don't think I'd better – someone might come in." Heather returned the pendant to its box and began to wrap it up again. "Besides, it wouldn't look right with an ordinary blouse. I shall keep it for special occasions."

"I think Dad meant you to wear it quite often," Judith said gently, wondering how many special occasions there were likely to be in Heather's life.

"Oh well – perhaps I will at home, but I don't approve of jewellery in the office so I certainly shan't deck myself in it during working hours."

The thought of Heather doing her domestic work with the pendant glittering on her rather flat bosom made Judith's lips twitch. She lived alone in a very small cottage on the outskirts of the village, a respected member of the community who "kept herself to herself" and had done it for so long that nobody took exception to it.

Dr. Corder would throw a fit if she didn't hurry back. Judith hastily searched for what she wanted in the filing cabinet and returned to the surgery. She thought no more about either Heather or her birthday present, and it was only recalled to her by her father's satisfaction expressed at lunchtime as he recounted his delivery of the pendant.

"The poor girl seemed quite overwhelmed – it was rather embarrassing, but I was glad you persuaded me to do it myself. I think she appreciated my taking the trouble to call in specially."

"I told you she would," Judith said absently, putting a plate down in front of him.

Her father looked up at her. "You've got a very thoughtful expression on your face. Did you have a difficult clinic this morning?"

She flung back her head and laughed outright. "I was only wondering what I would wear for the dance on Friday!"

Rodney joined in her amusement. "I'm glad you're going, dear. I never wanted you to cut yourself off from all your friends. I suppose Sean's coming here to fetch you?"

"Oh yes – about half-past seven. I hope surgery doesn't last too long because I shan't have a lot of time afterwards for getting ready. Hugh Renton's taking it and he's generally rather slow."

On Friday afternoon she washed her hair, drying it in the garden, and put her dress and everything else ready so she need waste as little time as possible after her bath.

The surgery was not very full but, as Hugh liked sometimes to devote half-an-hour to one patient if he thought it necessary, they did not move onwards at a very great pace. Nevertheless, the last of them was dealt with before seven o'clock, leaving plenty of time for Judith's transformation.

Unfortunately Hugh seemed inclined to talk.

"You're seeing quite a lot of Melanie, I believe," he said abruptly as Judith began her tidying up. "How do you think she seems?"

"Better, I think, but I sometimes wonder whether she ought to be so anti-social. Was she always inclined that way?"

Hugh considered, twirling a ballpoint pen round on the desk like a top. "I don't think so but I haven't seen much of her since she went to boarding school. I'm pretty sure it's only due to shock, and I'm hoping it will wear off."

"I expect it will." Judith picked up a collection of notes and began to sort them rapidly.

"I really am very grateful to you for letting her spend so much time at your house." Hugh looked up with great earnestness. "A girl that age is a terrible responsibility but I feel I owe it to my brother to do everything I can to help her through this difficult time."

"Yes, of course – it's only natural you should feel like that." She heroically avoided glancing at the clock. "I suppose it's a good thing really that Melanie's so grown up and doesn't seem to need friends of her own age. It makes everything much easier."

"She's certainly very little trouble – I think even Mrs. Crowfield would admit that." A rueful smile appeared suddenly on his serious face. "But I do wish she wasn't quite so fond of pop music!"

"It's a healthy liking," Judith pointed out, "and absolutely right for a teenager. Perhaps if she *didn't* like it, there might be more cause for concern."

"You could be right," he admitted, "and I suppose her 'tranny' is company for her when she's alone."

Judith agreed and avoided prolonging the conversation by not admitting that she enjoyed a background of pop music too and could quite understand Melanie's addiction to it.

The tidying up was finished and she reached for her shoulder bag while Hugh checked one or two items in his medical case. She had just started to say: "I'll be on my way now, doctor," when the telephone rang.

Hugh, still at the desk, put out his hand and silenced it immediately. "Dr. Renton."

Something made Judith pause in the doorway though there was no reason why she should.

A male voice at the other end crackled in a gruff staccato, and as Hugh listened a look of horror leapt into his eyes.

"On the bridge near Mill House? . . . Yes, I know it. Have you phoned for the police and the ambulance? . . . Oh yes, definitely – *at once.* I'll be there in about fifteen minutes."

He replaced the receiver and snatched up his case while Judith stood frozen in the doorway and stared at him.

"There's been a bad accident near Mr. Catchpole's house and I must get there as quickly as possible. You'd better come too."

"Yes, of course." Locking the doors as she came to them, she hurried after him as he strode out to his car. "Do you know any details?"

"Only that it's bad – and that a coach was involved. It went through the parapet of the bridge over the mill stream and overturned."

Another coach crash, and this time Hugh would be closely involved with the accident itself. Inevitably he would be reminded of that other one in France. Judith stole a look at his set face as they drove swiftly down the village longing to tell him she understood how he must be feeling.

Fortunately she guessed that any expression of sympathy would be unwelcome and wisely kept silent, occupying her mind instead with the problem of how she was to get a message to Sean explaining that she would be unavoidably delayed, that she might even not be able to go to the dance at all.

CHAPTER SIX

THE ACCIDENT had occurred about eight miles from Bedwell Green on a tree-lined stretch of rather narrow road which followed the windings of the River Dune and was popular with evening "mystery tours".

At one point the millstream joined the river, flowing between high banks to reach it and necessitating an awkward, rather picturesque bridge which was much photographed and sketched. Mr. Catchpole, busy in his garden a few yards upstream, had been a horrified witness of the disastrous meeting between a laden coach and a small car which had resulted in the coach ripping the parapet apart and crashing through to the water below.

The police car was already there when Hugh and Judith arrived. A patrol car was parked in the drive leading to Mill House and the doctor drew up behind it and leapt out.

"Nasty mess, sir," the policeman said tersely. "We're going to have a right job getting them out of there and up the bank."

Hugh went to the shattered bridge and looked over. The rear end of the coach was only just below him, but it was the wrong way up, with all the wheels and underneath part on view. Nevertheless, he was relieved to see several white faces looking out at him as their blood-streaked owners gesticulated frantically for rescue.

"The emergency door's jammed," the officer told

him, "and the ordinary door's under water. We'll have to smash the windows."

"Looks like several of them are broken already."

"Yes – bound to be with a jolt like that. But it's no use folks trying to climb out with jagged glass all round them. We've got to make a good job of it and clear a proper space, and until we've done that we shan't know how many's badly hurt inside."

More policemen had arrived by now and in the distance they could hear the sirens of approaching ambulances. Onlookers had appeared by magic, among them several able-bodied men, and in a remarkably short time a plan had been worked out for releasing the trapped victims of the crash.

Judith stood watching, longing to help and knowing that at this stage she could only be a liability. It was strength which was needed at present rather than medical knowledge, but there would be plenty for her to do as soon as they started bringing people out.

In the meantime, something temporarily forgotten was nudging the back of her mind and she suddenly realised that Sean still did not know what had happened. Perhaps she could phone from the house?

Quietly and unobtrusively she slipped away from the scene and ran up the drive. Mrs. Catchpole willingly showed her where the telephone was but it then occurred to her that it would be too late to ring the hospital – Sean would have already left – and there was no one at home at Grove Farm House and her father's calls were being switched through to another doctor.

It was then that she thought of Melanie. She surely wouldn't mind walking the short distance to the house and intercepting Sean at the gate. It really was necessary that he should be told about the accident.

"Hugh won't be coming home for hours and hours?" Melanie had seized on what, to Judith, was the least important aspect of the matter.

"He's going to be terribly busy here – "

"Are you helping him?"

"I certainly hope to, as soon as it's possible." Judith's voice took on a pleading note. "Melanie, *please* do what I asked. I don't want poor Sean hanging about wondering where on earth I've got to."

"Okay – I'll put the boy friend's mind at rest. Is he nice, Judy?"

"Yes, of course he is. Thanks a lot. I think I'd better hurry back now, in case I'm wanted."

She replaced the receiver and returned quickly to the scene of the accident, arriving just as the first victim was brought out – a young woman with cuts and bruises who was hysterical.

There was no sign of Hugh and she discovered that he had climbed into the wrecked coach and was working among the carnage inside, assessing injuries and directing those who were doing the rescue work.

After that Judith could not complain that she had nothing to do. Used as she was to distressing scenes in hospital, particularly when she had worked in the accident wards, she was sickened by the terrible injuries which some of the passengers had suffered.

Working beside one of the ambulance men, she mopped up, bandaged and comforted what began to seem like a never-ending stream – mostly female – of shocked and lacerated people with all sorts of fractured limbs.

"Surely they must be nearly all out now?" she said at last, addressing no one in particular during a brief lull.

"There were forty of us so I think there must be quite a lot more to come," a woman with a broken arm informed her from the seat on one of the garden chairs thoughtfully provided by Mrs. Catchpole. "A Mother's Union outing, that's what it was, and all I can say is – thank God we didn't have our children with us."

By now the ambulances were operating a shuttle service and Judith's informant was soon given a place in one of them. The short interval seemed to be over and the helpers were now – with the greatest difficulty – bringing out a stretcher case.

A middle-aged woman, she was conscious and talkative in spite of her serious injuries. "It's like hell in there," she told Judith, pausing to draw in great gulps of the fresh air. "That young doctor's doing a grand job, but what with the water and the blood and all that broken glass – to say nothing of having at least half-a-dozen that's passed right out – he's got his hands full and no mistake."

"Do you know what happened to the driver?"

"Dead, I shouldn't wonder – maybe drowned." She checked herself hastily and bit her lip. "I was going to say – serve him right, but that wouldn't be very Christian of me, would it?"

"It may not have been his fault." Judith began carefully to pick out pieces of glass from the tousled grey hair. "There was a car involved as well, you know." She did not add that the driver of this was suffering from nothing more than severe shock.

The ambulance men were ready to move her

patient – who still seemed totally unaware of the extent of her fractures – and Judith moved on to the next.

And so it continued; time had long ago ceased to exist and all thought of the very different evening which she had contemplated was completely erased from her mind as she laboured on. Totally absorbed, her white apron splashed with red and a streak of mud on one cheek, she was no longer aware of how many casualties she had tended, so that it was a surprise to discover suddenly that there were no more.

And yet they were still bringing out laden stretchers. The only difference that the figues on these were completely covered by red ambulance blankets.

"How many were killed, Nurse?" It was Mr. Catchpole who, with his wife, had unobtrusively assisted all the evening, providing cups of tea as well as chairs and sympathetic listening.

"I don't know." Judith was shaken by the sight of those still forms. "I – I didn't count."

"It does seem such a shame," put in Mrs. Catchpole. "They were having such a lovely drive and all enjoying themselves, and then this has to happen." She sighed and plodded wearily back to her house to make yet another pot of tea.

"Dr. Renton'll be glad to get out of there." Mr. Catchpole gazed down at the wreck. "I suppose when we see him we'll know it's finished at last."

As he spoke Hugh appeared at the glass-less window which had been used as an exit, and at the sight of him Judith gave an involuntary exclamation of distress.

His bare arms were bleeding from a multitude of

small cuts and his face was drawn, sweat-streaked and dirty, his hair wildly untidy and hanging over his eyes. Accepting a helping hand from a policeman, he dragged himself clear of the coach and somehow reached the bank and from there climbed to the bridge.

Judith moved quickly to meet him. "You look as though you could do with some first aid yourself." Deliberately she tried to make her voice sound as normal as possible.

His haunted eyes rested on her face for a moment. "I'm all right."

Mr. Catchpole came to join them. "You must feel you'd like a bit of a clean up, doctor, so why not come along to our house before you go back? The wife's just making fresh tea and I'm sure a cup wouldn't come amiss."

Brandy was what he needed by the look of him, Judith thought, but she did not say so. To her relief Hugh made no attempt to argue and, moving in a sort of trance, walked silently to the house, apparently quite unaware that Judith was carrying his medical bag.

"The bathroom's at the top of the stairs," Mrs. Catchpole said after one shocked look.

He went upstairs like a sleep-walker, followed by Judith. At the door she held out the bag.

"You'll probably need this."

He glanced at it and then down at his blood-streaked arms, appearing to notice them for the first time. "What a mess!"

"Do you want any help?" she ventured.

Hugh shrugged and then hesitated. "You'll probably make a better job of it than I shall." With an air of utter weariness, he subsided on to the bathroom stool.

Judith went to the washbasin and filled it with warm water, adding plenty of disinfectant. Slowly and gently, she cleaned up the abrasions, finding among them several deeper cuts which required plaster.

"Thanks." He rolled down his shirt sleeves and fumbled with the buttons.

"You ought to have an anti-tetanus injection."

"Yes, I suppose so."

He was making no attempt to stand up and Judith gazed at his white face in concern. He looked as though he might faint at any moment.

"Are you all right, Hugh?" she asked anxiously. "Is there anything else I can do?"

To her distress he bowed his head and put his hand over his eyes, making a strangulated, choking sound which was very like a sob.

"Oh God – I'm sorry to be such a fool, but it brought it all back to me – I keep remembering that crash in France – it was a coach too, you know. I'll never forget having to identify David and Sally – they'd tidied them up, of course, but it was still pretty grim."

Afterwards Judith could not think how it happened. Perhaps she had made a slight movement towards him, or maybe he was feeling so ill and tired and unhappy that the initiative came from him.

Whatever the beginning of it, she suddenly found that she was holding Hugh in her arms, his face pressed against her breast, while she stroked his tumbled hair as though he had been a child in distress.

Neither of them said anything. There was nothing to say. The need was for human contact and Judith had instinctively supplied it.

After a while Hugh straightened up. "Sorry about that."

His voice was curt but she understood how he felt at such a display of weakness, and was not resentful.

"You've had a terrible ordeal – it's natural you should be affected by it after – after the other," she said.

"It's no excuse at all." He got to his feet and produced a comb from his pocket. "I'd better make myself look a bit more presentable and then we'll go down and drink Mrs. Catchpole's tea." Briefly his eyes flickered over her face. "Did you know you've got mud on your cheek?"

In the living room he was very quiet but otherwise quite normal in his manner, and they left as soon as they decently could.

"I'd better get on with my evening calls," Hugh said as they walked down the drive.

Judith gave him an exasperated glance. "Do you realise what the time is?"

"I haven't given it a thought."

"It's half-past nine. Nobody will be expecting you now; they'll all be thinking about settling for the night."

He made an impatient gesture. "There are one or two I *must* see – people I'm worried about."

"Then why don't you go back and ring one of the other doctors? Dad wouldn't mind, I'm sure – " She broke off as he interrupted her angrily.

"When I want your advice, I'll ask for it!"

"Sorry!" She bit her lip, wondering that he could possibly be the same man who had clung to her for comfort in the bathroom.

Perhaps it hadn't really happened, maybe it was all part of the dreamlike nature of the evening.

But most of it had been much more of a nightmare, and a particularly terrible one at that. It was only the incident at the Mill House which had seemed like a dream, and a very beautiful one too.

"Are you in a hurry to get back?" Hugh asked abruptly as they got into his car.

Sean would have known that it was useless to wait for her. "Not particularly. Why do you ask?"

"Because three of my calls are between here and Bedwell Green and it would help if I didn't have to drive you home first."

"There's certainly no need to bother about me."

So Judith remained in the car while Hugh visited his patients, and found herself glad of the peaceful interlude, the soothing silence of the countryside. By the time they reached their own village it was nearly an hour later.

"I'll drop you off at your house and then make my last call," Hugh said.

He sounded much more like himself now, she was glad to notice. Perhaps the normal routine of his work had had a beneficial effect after all.

At Grove Farm House a light shone out from the hall and another from the study. Judith said "Good night" quickly and slipped out of the car.

"Thank you for all your help. I hope you didn't find it too distressing?" Hugh said.

"I'm a nurse and I ought to be able to take practically everything in my stride."

"You're human as well." He hesitated and then added so softly that she only just caught the words: "And so am I. One never gets really hardened – thank God."

Indoors Rodney greeted his daughter with relief. "I heard about the accident when I was on my rounds and thought you might have been involved instead of going to the dance. Was it very bad?"

"Horrible!" Judith gave him a brief outline of what had occurred, and he, understanding what it must have been like, did not press her for details.

"It's a pity you were disappointed over your outing," he remarked as they sat in the study with their bedtime drinks.

"I didn't have time to think about it. I suppose you didn't see anything of Sean?"

Her father shook his head. "I haven't been home myself very long. Were you able to let him know?"

Judith explained about the message entrusted to Melanie.

"That'll be all right then. He's sure to understand, being a doctor himself."

"I hope so." She sighed, suddenly overwhelmed with weariness. "But I'm afraid he'll be very fed up and I can't say I blame him." With a stifled yawn, she dragged herself to her feet.

"I'll come up too." Rodney put his glass down and followed her into the hall. "I'm pretty tired myself."

But the evening was not yet over.

Judith was putting away her evening dress and gold sandals when the telephone rang downstairs. Her father was taking a shower and so she hurried to answer it.

"Hugh Renton here." His voice was sharp and sounded very agitated. "Have you got Melanie at your house?"

"No – of course not. Is she supposed to be here?"

"I haven't a clue. All I know is that she's missing and Mrs. Crowfield hasn't seen her since early evening."

"I rang her up from Mill House and asked her to walk round here and give a message to – to a friend of mine who was expecting me to go to a dance with him this evening. That was about seven-fifteen."

"I didn't know you had a date," Hugh said, momentarily side-tracked. "You didn't tell me."

"There was no point in mentioning it."

"I'm sorry you had to miss it, though." He reverted quickly to his niece's disappearance. "Mrs. Crowfield says Melanie went out about that time but she gave no indication of where she was going. It must have been to take your message, but where on earth can she be now?"

Judith sought desperately for something to say which would allay his fears, but could think of nothing.

"Hang on a minute and I'll ask Dad if he saw her anywhere around."

He had just emerged from the shower when she put the question and at once declared that he had seen nothing of Melanie.

"I hope the silly girl hasn't done anything really foolish, Judy."

"I don't see why she should."

"Nor do I, but anything's possible with teenagers."

"I wonder if we ought to tell the police," Hugh

said despondently when Judith had relayed the information, or lack of it.

"It's a bit soon for that, surely?"

"Yes, I suppose it is. She'll probably come home soon and be surprised at all the fuss – and won't I tear her off a strip if she does!"

"You'll let us know?" Judith asked.

"No matter how late it is?"

"Yes, please."

He promised to do so and rang off, having completely banished all thought of sleep from Judith's mind, in spite of her father's urging.

"You'll be dead on your feet tomorrow, dear, and there's nothing you can do."

"I know there isn't but I feel responsible, in a way," she returned. "If I hadn't given her that message she probably wouldn't have gone out. There must be a connection."

"It's ridiculous to blame yourself – "

"Don't keep on at me, Dad – please!" Judith begged. "I wouldn't sleep even if I did go to bed. I'll curl up on the sofa and rest, maybe doze a bit, so don't switch the phone through to your bedroom, the way you usually do."

He gave up then and retired to his own bed, and Judith collected an armful of rugs and cushions and took them into the sitting room, leaving the hall light on so she could see her way to the study easily if the phone did ring.

As soon as she tried to settle down, the fears which she had been holding at bay rushed in triumphantly to the attack. It was now half-past eleven. There was no possibility at all that Melanie wasn't in some sort of trouble. Anything could have happened to her – *anything*!

Her thoughts flew to Hugh, keeping his vigil at Birch Cottage. He must be torturing himself with similar imaginings to her own and it wasn't fair – he'd been through enough lately without this added ordeal.

Staring into the half-darkness – she had left the door ajar – Judith tried to relax and found herself as rigid as ever. And yet she must have slipped into a state of semi-consciousness because when a car door shut noisily outside she jumped so violently that her heart started beating as fast as though she had been running a race.

She was on her feet and moving towards the front door without realising she had moved. Flinging it open, she gazed out into the dark night – and found Sean coming up the path.

CHAPTER SEVEN

"I SAW the light," Sean explained, "and I didn't think you would mind a late call." He stepped over the threshold, smiling and looking rather pleased with himself.

"What are you doing in Bedwell Green at this hour?" Judith looked up at him in bewilderment. "Is the dance over?"

"It finished at midnight. As for what I'm doing here, I had to drive Melanie home, didn't I?"

"You *what*?" Her voice rose in amazement. She could hardly believe that she had heard aright.

"When you let me down, Judy, I don't mind admitting I was hopping mad, though I could see that you didn't really have much option. And there was this girl – attractive and all that, and obviously at a loose end. So I took her instead. It's as simple as that."

"But – but," Judith put out a hand and grasped the back of the hall chair. "She's too young – "

Sean stared at her belligerently. "What d'you mean she's too young?"

"She's not even fifteen until September. Oh, I know she looks a lot more but – "

"Well, I'm damned!" His face showed a medley of emotions in which amusement dominated. "I didn't ask her her age, naturally, but I did refer to it obliquely during the evening and she didn't put me right. The little devil – fooling me like that! Not that it mattered much, for we got on fine together."

He moved nearer and put his hands on her shoulders. "I've quite got over being angry because you stood me up but I'd rather it had been you I took to the dance, Judy – make no mistake about that, love."

She felt no reaction to his touch and after a moment she slipped away. But it was impossible to go on being annoyed with him; it wasn't his fault that Melanie had behaved so outrageously.

"I'm sorry, Sean, but I'm just about all in," she apologised. "We were all terribly worried about Melanie's disappearance, and coming as it did on top of everything else – "

The telephone was ringing and she dived into the study to silence it.

"Yes, I know Melanie's safely back," she said quickly as soon as Hugh identified himself. "Sean just called in to tell me about it."

"I hope you gave him a piece of your mind," Hugh said grimly. "He ought to be shot, taking a kid of that age off to a grown-up dance without asking anybody's permission. He must have known she hadn't even left a message."

"I think perhaps he wasn't aware of that, or maybe he wouldn't think it necessary." Judith felt impelled to do her best for Sean. "And he seems to have judged Melanie's age by her appearance which, you must admit, is very deceptive."

"I'm not accepting that as an excuse. Melanie says quite definitely that she told him how old she was and all he said was 'So what?' You can tell your boy friend that he'd better keep away from my niece in future – and out of my sight – or I won't be answerable for the consequences."

"Very well," Judith said with a meekness she certainly was not feeling. Somebody just had to be lying and she was very much inclined to think it was Melanie, but Hugh wouldn't believe it even if she told him so; of that she was quite certain.

"Good-night." There was a sharp click as Hugh replaced the receiver.

Judith returned to the hall and gave Sean an edited account of the conversation. She was not surprised when he indignantly denied that Melanie had confessed to her real age.

"I'm not a baby-snatcher, Judy. I would never have taken her if I'd known, but she was wearing this long skirt, you see, and she looked at least eighteen."

That seemed to be where they came in, and Judith knew that she had had enough. By the time she had told her father about it – he had heard the telephone and come downstairs – and got rid of Sean, she was so exhausted that her own bed seemed the most desirable place in the world. Within five minutes of the final closing of the front door she was asleep.

But at Birch Cottage they took much longer to reach a state of mind which made sleep even a remote possibility.

"I'll accept that it was ninety per cent the boy's fault," Hugh said unhappily, "but the fact remains that you went off into the blue without letting anyone know. That wasn't good enough, Melanie."

To his astonishment she gave him a mutinous look and muttered sulkily: "I didn't think you'd care."

"Not care?" He could hardly believe his ears – and after he'd done his best to make her feel loved and wanted. "Of course I care what happens to you.

What on earth makes you imagine that I wouldn't?"

"You went to help at that accident without telling me, and you generally come home after surgery and have a meal. If Judy hadn't phoned I wouldn't have known anything about it." Melanie stole a peep at him from beneath her lashes. "*And* you took her with you though you never take me, except just that once when we went to Duneham."

"For heaven's sake! Judith is a nurse and was able to do a lot to help. It's completely different from taking somebody just for a ride."

But Melanie had made up her mind that she had a grievance and she maintained an obstinate silence, in spite of all Hugh's reasoning. He felt convinced she must know perfectly well that her attitude was ridiculous but apparently nothing would induce her to admit it. Eventually his patience was completely exhausted.

"I'm not going to talk about it any more," he told her flatly. "You'd better go to bed and let me do the same, and tomorrow I hope you'll be in your right mind again."

He had not expected an answer and was amazed at the one he received. Melanie suddenly tossed back her long hair and, her blue eyes drowned in tears, flung herself into his arms, clinging to him with a passionate intensity.

"Oh, Hugh, I'm sorry! I can't bear you to be angry with me and I'll never, never do anything again to make you so cross. And if Sean aks me to go out with him on another occasion I'll tell him I don't want to have anything to do with him – not ever!"

"If Judith conveyed my opinion of him correctly,

I hardly think he's likely to." Hugh held the slender sobbing form tightly and gave a great sigh of thankfulness because the rift between him and Melanie was apparently ended. Now perhaps he could salvage what remained of the night and get some sleep.

But it proved to be much more difficult than he had expected and he lay awake for a long time, seeing again the awful scene which had met his eyes when he climbed into the wrecked coach, and hearing in his imagination the heart-rending cries of the injured.

And every now and then he would remember the scene in the bathroom at Mill House, when he had made such a fool of himself. Judith had been very nice about it, but she must have thought him a terrible weakling to let his feelings get the better of him like that.

The best he could hope for was that she would forget it as soon as possible.

In the next room Melanie also was tossing and turning. She had been over-stimulated by her adventure and Sean's good-night kiss had made her cheeks burn with an emotion she did not understand. Perhaps he had fallen in love with her? After all, he hadn't know her real age until afterwards.

The lie she had told her uncle did not worry her at all because it had been in self-defence. Hugh's good opinion was far too necessary to her for it to be jeopardised by anything so unimportant as the truth, and she considered she had suffered quite enough scolding for going to the dance without permission.

Eventually she fell asleep from sheer exhaustion, and when Hugh dragged himself up in time for breakfast, she was still lost in deep and childish slumber.

"Don't disturb her," he said to Mrs. Crowfield. "She was very late to bed."

"Which was entirely her own fault."

"Yes, I know, but it's been all sorted out now and the subject is closed."

His landlady made no comment, but if he had been looking at her he would have noticed that her lips tightened.

"I hope you haven't forgotten that I shall be going away in a couple of weeks," she said when she brought in his coffee.

"As soon as that?"

"We break up next week and I'm off to Greece the week after. I *did* tell you some time ago."

"Yes, I remember, but I hadn't realised it had crept up on us so quickly." He paused to fill his cup. "Perhaps, in a way, it's a good thing. Melanie will have to learn to do a bit of housekeeping and that will keep her occupied."

It didn't seem to have occurred to him, Elizabeth thought wryly, that she might object to having a teenager messing about in her kitchen during her absence.

"It really would be much better if you could make other arrangements for her while I'm away," she told him.

Hugh glanced up at her in alarm. "I honestly don't think that's necessary, Mrs. Crowfield, and I wouldn't be able to think of anything even if I wanted to. We ought to be able to get on okay without you, and Mrs. Mayhew coming in to do all the cleaning. There'll only be the meals to get."

Only! Mrs. Crowfield repressed a smile and mentally shrugged her shoulders. Let them get on with it as best they could; she would be far away and wouldn't care – not until she returned, anyway. Deliberately she repressed another aspect of the matter which had been in her mind and retreated to the kitchen.

Two weeks later she packed her bags and departed and immediately Bedwell Green and Birch Cottage faded from her consciousness as completely as though they had never existed.

At first Melanie was delighted to have the opportunity to display her prowess in cooking, but several disasters eventually drove her to seek Judith's advice.

"How do you make pastry so it's not gooey to roll out?"

"By not putting so much water in it."

"But it won't stick together at all then."

"You have to judge it very carefully. Come into my kitchen and I'll try to give you a demonstration."

It was the first time Melanie had been to Grove Farm House since the night of the dance, and Judith was able to welcome her more cordially than she could have done earlier. She had been seriously annoyed about the lie which had put nearly all the blame on Sean, even though she understood the reason for it.

"When you get fed up with catering," she said, "you must let me know and I'll ask you and your uncle round here for a meal. I've had enough practice now to be able to produce something reasonably eatable."

"Could we come soon?" Melanie asked promptly.

"Yes, of course." Judith was startled at this wholehearted acceptance of her casual invitation. "How about next Saturday? It's my father's day off and he'd enjoy having people in to supper."

Rodney, when the subject was mentioned to him, immediately concurred. "Good idea, Judy. It will give poor Hugh a break, and the girl as well." He hesitated. "Could we ask one or two other people, do you think? Make it a sort of party?"

She had never had to cater for more than two so far ... Horrified but unwilling to admit it, Judith merely asked: "Like who, Dad?"

"Well, it's hard to say. I'd like to have Andrew Graham and his wife – I doubt if he ever gets a decent meal either – but I couldn't do that without having Corder as well – "

"Four doctors together! You'd never stop talking shop and Melanie would die of boredom."

"I wasn't seriously suggesting it, dear." Rodney hesitated again and then said diffidently: "I suppose we could invite Heather. It would be a good idea to give her a meal in return for several she's cooked for me in the past."

"I thought the pendant was partly for that," Judith commented before she could stop herself.

"Well, yes, in a way, but I think an invitation to supper would be a nice gesture."

There had been a slight stiffness in his tone and she tried to make up for her lack of enthusiasm.

"Would you like me to ask her then?"

"Thank you, Judy. It would be better coming from you. Perhaps you'd like to see if Sean can come as well? Then we'll have even numbers."

"Good heavens, Dad! – he'd be like a red rag to a bull where Hugh's concerned! I couldn't possibly include him."

Her father laughed. "I'd forgotten about the dance, but I can see that it wouldn't do."

As soon as they reached the surgery in the morning, Judith issued her invitation.

Heather looked up from her typewriter in astonishment and then dropped her gaze as the ready flush stained her cheeks.

"That would be lovely, Judith. I don't know when I last went out to a meal," she said with a surprising quiver of emotion in her voice.

"Don't expect too much – I'm not nearly such a good cook as you." In the doorway of the consulting room, Judith looked back. "By the way, Dr. Renton and his niece will be there too."

"That girl!" Heather bit her lip. "I'm sorry, I've got no reason at all for disliking her, except that I can't stand teenagers at any price. They're so full of their own importance and they don't know *anything*."

"We all have to go through that stage," Judith reminded her, trying to picture the secretary in those distant days and finding it utterly impossible. It seemed as though she must always have been grown-up and spinsterish.

"I'm sure we weren't so silly in my time," Heather said loftily.

"I bet people older than you said just the same sort of things that you've been saying about Melanie." Pleased that she had got the last word, Judith went into the consulting room and shut the door.

That afternoon she planned her menu and then

went along to the village shop to make some purchases. She was fortunate in finding the shop empty so that she had Mrs. Dixon's undivided attention, with the inevitable result that she soon found herself explaining why it was that she required tins of vichysoisse soup, and gelatine, and one or two other items not normally on her shopping list.

"Going to serve the soup chilled, are you, dear?" The shopkeeper sounded dubious. "To my mind that's a bit of a contradiction but I expect you know what you're doing, and you can always heat it up if the evening's cold. How many's it for?"

"Er – four or five, Mrs. Dixon." Knowing that she was expected to give the names, Judith felt reluctant to do so and compromised by not mentioning Heather.

"I don't think Dr. Renton and his niece are getting anything much in the way of appetising food with Mrs. Crowfield away," she finished. "Not that I'm much of a cook but I'm better than Melanie."

"It seems a funny business that girl still being here," Mrs. Dixon observed. "Not quite the thing, if you ask me."

Judith had had no intention of asking for her opinion, but she could not let such a remark go unchallenged and she exclaimed at once: "What on earth do you mean? Melanie is Dr. Renton's brother's child, so why in the world shouldn't she live with him? After all, he was left in charge of her, and I should have thought the fact that they're related made everything perfectly all right."

Mrs. Dixon looked doubtful. "Well, dear, it's not quite as simple as that, is it?"

Behind Judith the shop door opened and a family

on holiday came in, the children loudly discussing what flavour ice lolly they intended to buy. Further intimate conversation was obviously impossible and she paid for her own purchases and left.

She was puzzled by the shopkeeper's comments but not particularly concerned. Mrs. Dixon – the nicest of women – took a tremendous interest in all her customers and shared with them their joys and sorrows, apparently with equal enjoyment. But she did sometimes get things a bit twisted, due largely to her habit of jumping to conclusions rather too quickly.

It was difficult to guess what could have caused such a dark hint about Melanie and Hugh, and she soon dismissed it from her mind, concentrating on her supper party instead.

As Saturday drew near, she began to feel nervous and to wish that Sean could have been included as moral support.

Her guests were such an oddly assorted trio. Heather would be critical and Melanie bored, and Hugh and her father would talk about the practice all the time, and she herself would be nothing but a sort of cook-waitress.

Fortunately, the reality turned out to be surprisingly enjoyable. Melanie was in a good mood and frankly praised the food, and Hugh also ate with appreciation. Heather, the pendant glowing against a drab navy dress, was at first rather quiet and shy but eventually even she relaxed.

"You've given us a very nice meal," she told Judith at the end of it.

"The chocolate mousse wasn't as set as I would have liked."

"But it tasted delicious, and it's extremely difficult to get a mousse just the right consistency." Heather stood up and began to collect the plates into a pile. "Do let me help you wash up."

"There's really no need – "

But the secretary insisted and Judith gave in. In the kitchen they worked almost in silence, but she could not help observing that Heather seemed thoroughly at home and knew where everything was kept.

They returned to find Melanie curled up in front of the television set while Rodney and Hugh were deep in discussion of an article in *The Lancet*. From that moment the party seemed to disintegrate as though, without the meal to bind them together, the various members of it – except the two doctors – had become aware of how little they had in common.

It was a relief to Judith when at ten o'clock Heather announced that it was time she went home. At the same moment the telephone rang.

"I hope that doesn't mean I've got to go out," Rodney went off to answer it.

"It's your day off – you shouldn't be expected to," Heather said to his departing back view.

"Dad likes to keep in touch though," Judith reminded her.

"I know that! He's so conscientious – he never gives himself a proper break." Aware that she had spoken far too fervently, Heather broke off and flushed.

"He had a particular reason for not having his calls switched to another doctor today. Mrs. Winton's started in labour and he's worried about her.

She really ought to be having her baby in hospital but she insisted on staying at home."

"I hadn't realised the baby was on the way." Heather looked interested. "I've got a cottage at Park Farm, as you know, but it's so very isolated that I often don't see anybody from the farmhouse for days. I don't think I've spoken to Mrs. Winton since I paid the rent at the beginning of the month."

Rodney returned from the study. "Sorry, everybody," he announced, "but I'll have to leave you."

"Is it Mrs. Winton?" Judith asked.

"Yes. Laura Heal's not at all happy about the way things are going." He glanced at Heather. "I could give you a lift if you really want to get home now."

She accepted with alacrity, and Hugh tapped Melanie on the shoulder.

"Time we were off, too, love."

"Oh no – I've got to see the end of this film. Judy won't mind, will you?" She looked up beseechingly but her gaze almost instantly returned to the screen.

"Of course not. Stay as long as you like." Judith turned to Hugh. "Do you want to watch it too?"

"Heaven forbid! I see enough drama in my ordinary life without staring at it on the telly." He went over to the open french windows and looked out into the garden. "It's so peaceful here, and so comfortable. I can't think of anything I'd rather do than just sit here and talk quietly."

And Judith realised, with a stab of surprise, that she didn't really want to do anything else either.

CHAPTER EIGHT

THE SITTING room at Grove Farm House was a large room, stretching from front to back, where the french windows opened on to the lawn. It was a very warm evening, with the glow of sunset still brightening the western sky, and Judith and Hugh settled themselves in two comfortable chairs facing the garden.

Behind them the television set murmured confidentially to Melanie, seated on the floor only a few feet away, and – apart from an occasional scream or shot – did not intrude on their conversation.

"It's lovely here." Hugh leaned his head back and gazed with half closed eyes at the darkening scene. "Your father manages to keep his garden in very good shape."

"He spends all his spare time in it."

"Do you help him?"

"Sometimes."

"It must have made a lot of difference to his life, having you here." He paused, anxious not to venture too far. But it was impossible to resist the effect of the pleasant, peaceful atmosphere and the beauty of the night.

"I never knew your mother," he went on, "but I'm sure her loss must have been a crushing blow to him – and to you too, of course."

"I wanted to throw up my nursing and come home," Judith told him. "But Dad wouldn't let me."

"It would have been a pity not to have qualified."

"Yes, I know. I'm glad I stayed on now."

Silence fell on them for a while, but it was companionable rather than uncomfortable and eventually Hugh broke it.

"That night the coach crashed – I'm not sure if I ever thanked you properly for all you did. And I didn't tell you either how sorry I was afterwards when I discovered you'd missed a date because of it."

"It didn't matter all that much."

"But you must have been disappointed, and I don't suppose it made things any better when you discovered that Melanie had gone in your place. I – er – hope it didn't lead to trouble with your boy friend?"

"Oh no." Desperately Judith wanted to explain that Sean wasn't her boy friend in any serious sense, but before she could think of the right words, the film which Melanie was watching suddenly became much more noisy.

There was a burst of gunfire and a lot of shouting, and Hugh stood up with a rueful smile.

"Sounds as though things are coming to a climax!" He moved over to the doorway and stood looking out into the shadows and Judith got up too and joined him.

Owls were calling to each other in the distance, and from the hedgerows came the agitated twitter of sparrows not yet settled for the night. A dog was barking on one of the farms, but the small sounds of Nature seemed only to emphasise the quietness which lay like a canopy over the garden immediately in front of them.

"I can't understand why some people don't like to hear owls." Hugh stepped down on to the lawn. "I'm rather fond of them myself. When I was a small boy I used to lie in bed, very warm and comfortable, and listen to the owls crying. We had a lot in the trees in our garden and they kept up quite a racket sometimes."

"Where was your home?" Judith asked as they left the noise of the television set behind them and began to stroll across the grass.

"In the Cotswolds. It's been my favourite part of the country ever since." He hesitated and then continued rather diffidently. "After my mother married again we lived in London – which was very different – but I was away at school by then and didn't mind all that much. When she departed to Australia, I'd already started my medical training and work became more important than a settled background."

He broke off and laughed in rather an embarrassed way. "Sorry to bore you with my family history instead of spouting poetry about the beauty of the evening!"

"If you suddenly started to quote poetry I should probably think you'd gone mad!" Judith joined in his amusement. "And I wasn't a bit bored. I think it's interesting to learn about people, but I'm not sure I agree with you that work is more important than a person's home."

"I didn't say that exactly. In fact, my opinion is that they're equally important. But if you haven't a proper home, then it's a good thing to be absorbed in your work."

"I should think you're quite comfortable at Birch Cottage, aren't you?"

"It's ideal for a bachelor, but I shall have to find somewhere else when Melanie leaves school. Mrs. Crowfield wouldn't want her there all the time."

"But she might not *be* there. Presumably she'll want to be trained for some sort of work."

"Well, yes, perhaps." Was it her imagination or did his tone seem suddenly evasive? "Actually, my brother left her very well provided for and it's a long time before any decisions need be taken – two or three years. A lot can happen in that time."

Judith agreed that it could be and they walked on in silence. Her feet in open sandals were rapidly becoming wet with dew but she neither noticed nor cared.

A strange mood had taken possession of her. It was almost as though the loveliness of the summer night had combined with the piercingly sweet scent of her father's tobacco plants to produce a kind of ecstasy of light-headedness.

She would have liked to go on walking indefinitely under the darkening sky, but inevitably they soon came to the hedge which bordered the fields and were obliged to turn back. And as they did so interruption arrived noisily and violently.

The film had ended and Melanie had awakened from her trance to find herself alone. She came hurtling out into the garden and her voice split the silence with a slightly hysterical note in it.

"Hugh! Where are you? I can't see you anywhere! Hugh!"

He answered her quietly. "Here I am – not twenty yards away, so there's no need to make such a racket."

"I was frightened." She raced across the grass and

slid her arm through his. "That film was terribly scarey at the end."

"Why did you watch it, then?"

"I couldn't stop myself and actually I enjoyed it enormously except the last bit. Shall we go home now?"

"It's certainly high time we did." He glanced at Judith, walking silently on his other side. "Goodness knows when your father will be back. Do you mind being on your own?"

"It's happened before! Actually I don't mind it at all in the summer, and I don't suppose I shall in the winter either, with the doors all safely locked."

They walked together round the house to where Hugh's car was parked.

"It seems daft to drive such a short distance," he remarked as he opened the door for Melanie, "but I thought I might be called out."

Judith murmured a suitable reply but afterwards she had no memory of what she had said. Some of the magic of that peaceful stroll in the garden still clung to her in spite of Melanie's intrusion, and when her guests had driven away she went back to the lawn and spent several minutes gazing dreamily at the stars and allowing her thoughts to wander where they felt inclined.

But the direction which they took was so disturbing that she hastily pulled herself together and went into the house and to bed.

Her father did not return until five o'clock in the morning. He was very careful but Judith, who had slept lightly, heard him and slipped out of bed. He would be tired and hungry after such a long night and perhaps would like an early breakfast.

"I didn't mean to disturb you." Unshaven, Rodney looked a good deal more tired than he was actually feeling. He accepted an offer of food and settled down at the kitchen table to talk about his case.

"I knew Mrs. Winton ought to have gone into hospital and I was right. If she hadn't been a week premature I might have been able to talk her into it. She had a very difficult labour but we won in the end, I'm glad to say."

"You mean you and Laura?"

"That's right. We've both been at it all night. Poor Nurse Heal looked flaked out and I told her to go home and get some sleep. The relief nurse will have to do her round this morning."

"She's on holiday."

"Is she?" Rodney took a sip of coffee. "It's funny Laura didn't mention it."

"Perhaps she was too tired to remember at the time." Judith turned round from the cooker. "Could I help at all? I know I'm not supposed to trespass on the district nurses' duties but this seems to be an emergency."

Her father considered the suggestion for a moment. "There's one snag, dear, and that's transport. You don't drive and in any case there's no car available."

"There's my bike – "

"My dear girl, it would take hours!"

"It's all the district nurses had at one time, Dad. I'm sure I could do the nearest calls on it, anyway."

But he shook his head. "I think we'd better let the nurses sort it out for themselves. Tell you what, though – you could call on Mrs. Winton for me. I'm very anxious she should have a nurse looking in as soon as possible and it's not very far."

He rattled off a list of medical instructions which Judith noted down with a pleasant sense of being of real use. After another brief period in bed she set off on her bicycle shortly after eight o'clock.

She had always liked babies and her time on the maternity ward at St. Helen's had been a happy one. She looked forward to making the acquaintance of the new member of the Winton household.

The farmhouse was old and oak-beamed, and with a tidy, prosperous yard. The Wintons were in their late thirties and had almost despaired of having a family; consequently the arrival of Anthony Thomas seemed very like a miracle.

Judith found Mrs. Watson looking pale and exhausted and yet radiant. She accepted her arrival without surprise and proudly displayed the baby.

"Isn't he lovely!" Leaning over the cot from her bed, she gazed down in rapture at her infant son. "Just look at his tiny fingers – he's quite perfect in every detail."

To Judith the baby looked terribly, pathetically frail. He slept peacefully, his rosebud mouth closed and the fair lashes lying still, but his breathing was almost imperceptible. He was very small too, though only seven days premature, and when she picked him up he seemed little more than a bundle of clothes.

At St. Helen's babies like this were put in an incubator until their hold on life strengthened.

"I expect you'd like to try and feed him," she suggested.

Mrs. Winton looked surprised. "Isn't it a bit soon? I thought the milk didn't come in yet."

"That's quite right, but there should be something for him, and besides it's a good idea for him to get the idea of sucking."

But Anthony Thomas remained entirely unco-operative and slept as peacefully as before, making absolutely no attempt to provide the stimulus which his mother's breast needed.

"I thought babies sucked instinctively," Mrs. Winton raised anxious eyes. "He doesn't seem a bit interested."

"I expect he's tired." Judith held out her arms. "I'll put him back in his cot and you can try again later."

"Not yet, Nurse. I believe he nearly opened his eyes then. Let me hold him a little longer – please."

She was looking worn out herself, and Judith began to worry in case she had been wrong in coming so early. And yet she hadn't disturbed her patient from sleep; she had been wide awake and her husband was already out and busy on the farm.

"There! He almost sucked then."

It was wishful thinking in Judith's opinion, but she did not argue about it. Their heads very close together, both of them leaned over the baby, anxiously willing the tiny fragile creature to make one more effort.

Neither of them heard a car door slam outside in the yard. The first they knew of Laura Heal's arrival was a head in a district nurse's cap poked round the door.

Judith swung round in astonishment. She had

believed Laura to be at home, snatching a few hours' sleep, and the sight of her was a shock.

"What's going on here?" The nurse's voice was ominously quiet. "I was under the impression that this was my case."

Mrs. Winton had fortunately been too absorbed in her baby to notice the animosity which had sprung up and she exclaimed in relief: "Perhaps you can get this little chap to suck, Nurse Heal. He just doesn't seem to want to make the effort."

"I don't blame him, seeing the struggle he had to get into the world." Laura deftly whisked the baby out of his mother's arms and back into the cot. "Let him sleep a bit longer and then he'll feel more like it."

"That's a good idea!" Mrs. Winton subsided against her pillows. "Nurse Lidgate seemed to think he ought to feed as soon as possible."

There were several comments which Judith would have liked to make but she kept them to herself. Two nurses arguing in front of the patient was unthinkable. She would save her defence until later.

"There's no need for both of us to be here." She smiled as cordially as she could manage and took off her mask. Rolling her sleeves down, she made for the door. "I'll be on my way, Mrs. Winton."

She was seething with annoyance as she went out to the yard where her bicycle was leaning against the wall, and she was not displeased to find that Laura had followed her on the pretext of fetching something from her car.

"I think you owe me an explanation," the district nurse said crisply. "I know you're a qualified nurse but it's news to me that you've taken midder."

"You're quite right – I haven't." Judith stared back at her defiantly. "But there's no need to get so steamed up. My father was worried about Mrs. Winton and the baby, and he asked me to look in because he thought you'd be getting some sleep."

"For your information *I* was worried too. I wouldn't have minded the interference so much if you hadn't been upsetting my patient by insisting on trying to get the baby to feed."

"At St. Helen's we always got the mothers to put the babies to the breast as soon as they were washed and dressed. Maternity Sister was very keen on it."

"I've nothing against it," Laura conceded, "in normal circumstances, though I don't think it's necessary. But this case is different. In my opinion the Winton baby will probably have to be sent to hospital. He's too frail to be handled at home."

"So you have *some* use for St. Helen's?" Judith snapped, and then felt annoyed with herself because it had sounded so childish.

"Of course I have!" Laura swung round on her heel and returned to the house.

Judith relieved her feelings by pedalling back at considerable speed. Dr. Graham, who was taking surgery that morning, had already arrived and she hastily explained her non-appearance at the proper time.

"I was late myself," he told her, running a hand through his thin gingerish hair and looking harassed, as he nearly always did. "My wife fancies the children are sickening for something and I had to take their temperatures before I left home."

"Do *you* think they are?"

"It's possible they've got a mild dose of this summer flu that's about just now." He smiled rather ruefully. "It had better not be anything serious because we're off on holiday in two or three weeks. Have you had your own holiday yet?"

"Dad and I are going to Scotland in October. Are you ready for the first patient?"

It turned out to be a small boy named Kevin who looked pale and listless.

"It's not like him at all," his mother told them. "So I thought he ought to have a check-up."

Dr. Graham was good with children and he gave the child a thorough examination, after which he took a blood sample.

"Nice little chap," he said to Judith when they were alone for a moment. "I hope to God I'm wrong in my diagnosis."

"What do you suspect, then, doctor?" she asked anxiously.

"It could be leukaemia." He sighed. "It sometimes comes on with horrifying suddenness and he has a lot of the symptoms. But, of course, I may be completely mistaken. There are other diseases which can be confused with it at this stage."

Judith felt a wave of depression wash over her, just as it had frequently done when she was in her first year of nursing, before she had learnt to be objective.

This was what ordinary practice did to you; somehow you were closer to the patients than in hospital, in spite of not doing so much for them. For one thing so few of them were strangers – Kevin lived in the white cottage near the duck-pond and she often saw him going to school. When you knew people, and their families, it was impossible to stand aloof, to be sympathetic but uninvolved.

With an effort she shook off her black mood and went to call the next patient. But unfortunately it turned out to be the kind of day when one depressing thing happens after another.

At the clinic which followed surgery, she had to tell one of the young mothers who had had a "smear" done that the doctor would like to see her.

"There's absolutely nothing to worry about," she insisted, but she could see that Mrs. Pilgrim did not believe her.

"How can you say that, Nurse!" the patient reproached her. "You know as well as I do that I've got cancer." Tears filled her eyes and she blinked furiously.

"It may not be that at all, and even if it is you'll almost certainly recover completely by getting it treated as quickly as this. That's the whole point of having a smear done."

Mrs. Pilgrim sniffed and made a great effort to appear composed. "I expect you're right, but I never thought it would happen to me."

"People never do think that," Judith said gently.

By the time Mrs. Pilgrim left, she had managed to instill in her a much more optimistic viewpoint. Nevertheless, the incident – which she knew she ought to have taken in her stride – added to the depression which she felt all day. It hardly seemed possible that only the previous evening she had been so happy.

When her father came in to lunch, he too seemed abstracted, and Judith was not surprised when he told her that he had had to send Mrs. Winton and her baby to hospital.

"It's the only chance the poor little fellow's got – and I blame myself for not insisting on hospital delivery in the first place."

"You weren't to know that she'd go into labour early – "

"What difference does that make?" He spoke with unusual irritability. "I should have put my foot down a month ago at least."

He ate his meal in silence, but before he went out again he unburdened himself of another disturbing matter.

"You know those three spinster sisters of Mrs. Bradbury's who live in that row of cottages opposite the shop?"

"Of course I know them!" Judith smiled. "They're so old-fashioned that they look as though they'd stepped straight out of Dickens."

"Their outlook is equally out-of-date," Rodney said crossly. "I stopped at the shop to buy a new ballpoint pen and when I came out they were standing round my car like the Three Fates. And what do you think they wanted? To complain because Hugh and Melanie are living at Birch Cottage without Mrs. Crowfield to chaperone them!"

"How absolutely absurd!" Judith said scornfully. But into her mind there flashed the memory of her conversation with Mrs. Dixon. She, too, had implied that the situation at Birch Cottage wasn't quite all it should be. "I hope you gave them a piece of your mind," she finished.

"I did speak out rather plainly," he admitted. "I shouldn't be surprised if they come to the surgery in a body and ask to be transferred to Corder's list."

They both laughed, though neither of them thought it particularly funny, and soon afterwards Rodney retired to the study for a short nap before starting his afternoon round.

Judith spent the afternoon doing the family laundry and then putting in an hour or so in the garden, by the end of which time she was feeling rather more at peace with herself.

And then, in the evening, she had a telephone call from Stella which put all the village news and views out of her head, and in a matter of seconds whisked her mentally back to St. Helen's.

"I thought I ought to let you know, Judy," Stella said, "that Sean is ill. He's in the side ward of men's surgical and I'm afraid it's serious."

CHAPTER NINE

"SEAN ILL?" Judith gasped. "Oh, Stella – how awful! What's the matter with him?"

"It *could* have been quite an ordinary case of appendicitis," Stella told her, "but you know what idiots doctors are about looking after themselves. Apparently it blew up very suddenly, the way it does sometimes, and Sean just thought it was indigestion."

"You mean he did nothing about it at all?"

"I expect he took some magnesia or bismuth or something and probably made himself feel a lot worse. Anyway, by the time he woke up to the truth the abcess had burst – "

"Then he's got peritonitis?"

"I'm afraid so. He was found collapsed in his room and operated on this morning, and nobody's been allowed to see him, of course, but Mary Stevens is a staff nurse on that ward and she says he's running a very high temperature."

"I'm not surprised," Judith said grimly. "Supposing he hadn't been found in time – he might have died!"

"He certainly might," Stella agreed soberly. "And it would have been his own fault."

Judith shuddered away from the picture of Sean lying alone and desperately ill, and tried to fasten on to something more cheerful. "He'll be all right, won't he, Stella? With modern drugs – "

"Oh yes, of course he will, but I didn't think

you'd want me to wait until he was better before letting you know what had happened. You'll come and see him, won't you?"

"I'll be there as soon as he's allowed visitors. Have they sent for his mother?"

"Mary says she's arriving this evening – it's a long way apparently – but she'll have to get back as soon as possible because of the children and her husband having been ill not long ago. She doesn't want to put too much on him."

"I'll wait until she's returned home and then visit Sean. And in the meantime, I'll keep in touch." Judith faltered a little. "If – if anything awful did happen – I mean, if he took a turn for the worse or anything, you'd give me a ring, wouldn't you?"

"Of course I would, you twit! But I hope you're not going to start torturing yourself with what *might* happen."

Having assured her friend that she wouldn't be so silly, Judith replaced the receiver and proceeded to do exactly that.

A man had died of peritonitis on that same ward; she remembered it perfectly from her early nursing days, and although he had been elderly and – for some reason – resistant to drugs, she couldn't help being depressed by the recollection.

She ought to have asked if Sean was on the dangerously ill list, just in case Stella had been exaggerating a little. But when she telephoned the hospital and was told that he was, she almost wished that she had not done so.

The news in the morning was no more cheering and Judith spent an anxious day, although she was temporarily gladdened by a very forthright apology which she received from Laura Heal when they met for a few minutes.

"I'm sorry I was rude to you yesterday. I hope you'll put it down to an almost sleepless night."

Very willing to meet her halfway, Judith assured her that of course she quite understood, but the district nurse had not yet finished.

"I realised afterwards that your father had asked you to call entirely for my benefit and I was more than ever sorry that I'd snapped at you."

"Forget it!" Judith was beginning to feel uncomfortable and she changed the subject lightly.

"How did Mrs. Winton react to having to go to hospital after all?"

"I think she was far too worried about the baby to think of herself. Her husband was the one who made the most fuss, but men usually do, of course."

Disentangling her car keys from a number of odds and ends in her pocket, Laura continued: "Life's oddly arranged, I often think. There's Mrs. Read at Manor Farm cottages – she has a baby every year and they come into the world as easily as kittens, *and* thrive right from the start. They're all greatly loved, naturally, but I can't feel that any of them are quite as precious as poor little Anthony Thomas Winton."

With a wave of her hand she departed and Judith began her own work. She had no difficulty in keeping her mind on it, but as soon as she left the surgery her thoughts returned to Sean. With an effort she made herself wait until evening before phoning, only to be told that he was "as well as could be expected", which left her very little wiser.

It was the same the following day, but the day

after that there was good news. Stella rang up to say that Sean was definitely better and she had actually seen him for a few minutes.

"His mother is going back tomorrow, Judy, and he was asking rather pathetically if you knew he was ill. I said you did and then he wanted to know why you hadn't been to see him. I don't think he realises how bad he's been."

"I hope you told him I would come soon?" Judith was distressed that Sean was apparently misjudging her.

"Yes, of course I did. Can you manage it tomorrow?"

"I think so – in the afternoon. Evening visiting is impossible because there's no bus."

Having arranged with her father – who was fortunately taking surgery – that she would be a little late, Judith went out the next day to stand at the bus stop outside Mrs. Dixon's shop.

She had not been there more than a few minutes when a car drew up in front of her and Melanie wound down the passenger's window.

"Are you going to Cumberton, Judy?"

Hugh was at the wheel and he leaned forward to look up at her. "We can give you a lift if you like. It'll be much quicker than by bus."

It was his day off, Judith remembered, and no doubt he was taking his niece out somewhere. "Thanks a lot." She got in the back and sat down. "I'm visiting a friend in hospital."

"Snap! I'm going to see a patient who's also a friend," Hugh engaged first gear and the car moved off.

Out of the corner of her eye, Judith saw three

wrinkled faces peeping from behind the curtains at the cottages opposite. Mrs. Bradbury's sisters didn't miss much.

"Mr. Macintosh has been in the geriatric ward at St. Helen's for over a month," Hugh went on, "and they don't seem to know what to do with him. He wants to come home, but unfortunately the old chap isn't fit to look after himself."

"Isn't that a matter for the social services to sort out?" Judith asked.

"Probably, but I don't want him to feel he's been consigned to hospital and then forgotten, so I thought I'd look him up – bring him the village news and all that."

"That's very kind of you," Judith said warmly.

"It's all part of the job – "

"It isn't, you know. Most doctors would think they couldn't spare the time." Sensing that her praise was making him feel thoroughly uncomfortable, Judith turned to Melanie. "Are you visiting Mr. Macintosh too?"

"Gosh – no! I don't like hospitals. Hugh's dropping me off at the library and I'm going to stock up with all the books they'll let me have. I always seem to have read all the ones they bring on the van. After that we're going out to tea at Coopers', where they have those super cream buns."

"Greedy!" Hugh laughed and turned his head to glance at her affectionately.

"You like them too!"

"You bet I do! But I daren't indulge the way you do. Nothing you eat seems to affect that lovely slim figure of yours."

"Or give me spots," Melanie said complacently.

Judith sat alone in the back listening to their continued bantering and, for some extraordinary reason, found herself beginning to feel completely out of it. Neither of them had given her any cause – they had both been perfectly friendly – and yet it seemed to her that she was of no more significance to them than a parcel on the back seat would have been.

But why on earth should she expect to be significant? What was the matter with her that she should let her imagination run away with her in such a ridiculous manner?

Resolutely she switched her attention off the conversation in front and stared out at the countryside. Harvest had already begun and straw bales were casually piled in many of the fields. Their clear outlines had a strange angular beauty which reminded her in some odd way of Stonehenge.

A column of black smoke rising in the distance caused Melanie to exclaim: "Oh, look – there's a fire! Can we go round that way and see what's burning?"

Hugh glanced in the direction she had indicated. "They're probably burning stubble and you'll be able to see plenty of that around Bedwell Green in the next few weeks."

"Why do they do that?" she asked in surprise.

"To get rid of it in the easiest way, of course."

"Does the fire ever get out of control?"

"Very rarely, and then usually because the wind has changed direction or sprung up suddenly. And, I suppose, just occasionally it's because somebody's been careless."

They left the fields behind them and came to the outskirts of Cumberton, and soon they were dropping

Melanie in the town centre and driving on towards the hospital.

"Thanks for the lift." Judith got out in the car park and looked up, to find Hugh staring down at her with a curiously intent gaze.

"How are you getting home?" he asked.

"By bus, of course. There's one soon after five."

"That's a long time to wait. Why don't you come back with us? We're leaving about four-thirty." Before she could answer, he went on rather hurriedly: "In fact, I've got a better idea than that. Come and have tea with us – I'm sure you like cream buns too."

"I adore them!" Judith broke into a smile but almost immediately became serious again. "Perhaps you wouldn't want to invite me if you knew whom I'm going to visit."

Hugh looked puzzled. "Sounds intriguing! Why on earth shouldn't I?"

"It's Sean – the boy who took Melanie to the dance. He's been very ill."

"My heart bleeds for him!" Hugh broke off and bit his lip. "Sorry – I shouldn't have said that. I wouldn't want the poor bloke to be ill, even if he did annoy me considerably, and you've got a perfect right to visit anyone you please. Besides, everything that happened on that night is supposed to be forgiven and forgotten."

"So the invitation still stands?" Judith asked lightly.

"Of course it does! Meet us at Coopers' about three-forty-five." With long strides he went off in the direction of the new geriatric wards.

On the way up to men's surgical it occurred to Judith that she was rather early for afternoon visiting and Sean might be having a nap. Accordingly, she went along to the maternity block via the bridge which linked it to the older part of the hospital to ask after the Winton baby.

"He's holding his own," the staff nurse told her, "but we're still having feeding difficulties. His mother's milk never got really established, unfortunately, so she'll be discharged any day now. But the infant will have to remain here. Would you like to go and look at him through the glass panel?"

Anthony Thomas looked, if anything, even smaller than he had when she last saw him. Judith gazed at his tiny form in dismay – she had, quite unreasonably, expected a miracle – and then turned away. He was in good hands, that was for sure, and she must leave him there and concentrate instead on the main reason for her visit to St. Helen's.

Returning slowly across the bridge – for it was still early – she looked about her, absorbing the familiar atmosphere, searching for well-known faces among doctors and nurses whom she passed and occasionally exchanged a greeting.

Every step held memories for her, some painful, some amusing, and all nostalgic. One moment the past seemed so close that she felt it must still be going on and she a part of it, and the next it receded so far that she could scarcely believe that it had ever happened.

She came to men's surgical and approached the small side ward, and the trance in which she had been moving fell away from her and once more her thoughts were all of Sean.

The door was half open and a murmur of voices halted her on the threshold.

"Hullo, Judy!" Someone spoke suddenly from the corridor and Judith spun round to find the staff nurse Mary Stevens smiling at her. "I'm glad you've come to see Sean because his mother is just going."

They entered the room together and Judith saw a small grey-haired woman with a worried expression sitting by the bed. Her eyes switched to the patient and, although she had been prepared for a change in him, his thin cheeks and hollow eyes shocked her so much that she was momentarily bereft of words.

Mary was speaking again. "Never a dull moment, Sean! Here's your girl friend arriving dead on cue to take your Mum's place at your bedside."

Mrs. Hargreaves, who had been searching for something in her handbag, raised her eyes quickly and looked at Judith. There was astonishment in them, and apprehension too, and they were still there when she turned her head to glance at her son.

But Sean was smiling lazily at the new arrival and took no notice.

The incident was so small and so swiftly ended that Judith was scarcely aware of it at the time, and yet she must have stored it in her memory because she remembered it later on, and understood.

She exchanged a smile and a polite murmur with his mother and then Mrs. Hargreaves stood up.

"I must be off, dear, or I'll miss my train." She laid some stamps on his locker. "You've no excuse for not writing letters now you're feeling so much better, so don't forget." An unemotional kiss landed on his forehead and, with another rather mechanical smile at Judith, she went quietly out of the room.

Sean held out his hand, the long fingers already thin and pale. "Come and say hullo properly now that we're on our own."

He clutched at her arm, his touch feeling hot and dry, and she bent her head to kiss him in much the same restrained way as his mother had done.

"How are you really, Sean? We were all so worried about you."

"I was a bit bothered myself," he admitted ruefully, "but not until I was over the worst. You don't realise at the time how ill you are, not even when you're supposed to be clued up about that sort of thing."

He was still holding her hand and Judith sat down in the chair his mother had vacated. Gently she tried to release her fingers, but his grip was strong and she was obliged to give up the attempt.

Sean chattered on, giving her a full description of his experience – as much as he could recall – with plenty of medical detail, and Judith, realising how much he was enjoying it, did not try to interrupt.

"It's wonderful to have a visitor who understands what I'm on about. My mother – bless her – didn't really take in a word," he finished at last.

"Everything you've told me boils down to one thing," Judith said severely. "You're a complete idiot when it comes to looking after yourself."

"I never thought – "

"But you should have thought! A doctor *needs* to take care of his own health – he owes it to his patients."

"That hardly applies to me," Sean persisted. "I'm not in general practice."

"You might be one day, so you ought to get into the habit now."

He looked at her soberly. "I'll never have enough money to become a G.P. It'll have to be hospital jobs for me for ever and ever. My folks aren't like yours, Judy – they're working-class people. Mum and Dad left school at fourteen and they've never had time to catch up with the education they missed."

"They must be very proud of you."

A faint colour stained the invalid pallor of his cheeks. "I reckon they are, though Mum doesn't hesitate to tear me off a strip when she thinks I need it."

"Have you ever thought of returning to your own city and getting a job at the hospital there?" Judith asked.

"What?" It almost seemed as though she had not heard the question and his face suddenly looked blank.

She was about to repeat it when, to her dismay, Sean released her hand and drooped against his pillows with an air of complete exhaustion.

"Pour me out a glass of water, Judy love – I feel a bit shattered."

"You've been talking too much." She stood up and did as he had asked.

"More likely it's the excitement of seeing you."

"Then I'd better go. It's obviously too much for you."

"No, no – I'm okay now." He drained the glass and put it back on his locker. "I wish they'd supply patients with beer; I'm sure it would do more good."

Judith re-seated herself and began to steer the

conversation into the safe channels of hospital gossip. After half-an-hour had passed she stood up resolutely and announced that she was not staying any longer.

"You'll come again?" Sean begged.

"How much longer will you be here?"

His expression clouded. "Maybe a week, and then they say I've got to go to Rowanheath to convalesce. I can't go home, you see, at first because Mum's got enough to do now."

"It's a very nice convalescent home – "

"It's ruddy awful! I had to visit a patient there once, and there wasn't a patient under fifty. I reckon I probably won't survive."

Judith laughed and then sobered abruptly as an idea struck her. Sean looked so forlorn that she felt really sorry for him and, being young herself, she could quite understand how he felt about Rowanheath.

Without stopping for further consideration, she put her idea into words.

"Would you like to come and stay with us when you leave here? I'm sure the hospital would approve, since Dad is a doctor."

"Could I? Oh, Judy darling, it would be heaven!" He was so pleased and still so physically weak that, for a moment, emotion almost overwhelmed him. "I wouldn't be any trouble – I promise you. I'd just lie in the garden all day. You'd only have to feed me."

"And that, I'm sure, would be quite an undertaking, judging by the look of you!" Judith smiled at him affectionately, delighted that she had pleased him so much. "I'll leave it to you to fix it with the hospital and you can let me know when I come to see you again."

His radiant face remained with her as she left the side ward, and it was some time before she allowed herself to wonder whether she really should have let her heart rule her head, whether there mightn't be a danger that Sean would read more into the invitation than simple kindness.

CHAPTER TEN

"WHAT ARE we waiting for?" Melanie stood outside the tea-shop, her arms full of books, and looked up at Hugh. "I'm starving!"

"I asked Judith to join us. She's meeting us here."

She stared at him incredulously. "Whatever made you do that? I thought this was supposed to be *my* treat."

Hugh bit back an impatient exclamation. "I expect there'll be enough cream buns to go round."

"But I wanted it to be just the two of us. You've never had time to take me out to tea before." Tears of disappointment rose into her eyes.

"I think you've forgotten that Judith gave us both a very good meal only last Saturday," Hugh said quietly. "It seemed a lucky opportunity to repay a little of her hospitality. And she's been very kind to you, letting you go round there just when you feel like it."

"I hardly ever go now."

"But you did when you first came." He put his fingers under her chin and tilted her face upwards. "Stop behaving like a spoilt brat, Melanie, for goodness' sake."

"How can I help it when you treat me like a child?" She wrenched her head away, and the topmost book slipped sideways and would have fallen to the ground if Hugh had not caught it.

"That's not the the way to treat library books," he scolded her. "Let me take some of them for you."

By the time they had divided the pile between

them, Judith had arrived and Melanie had apparently recovered from her sulkiness.

Tea was a pleasant meal with the conversation handled lightly and controversy avoided. They discussed Mr. Macintosh, who had announced his intention of returning to his cottage whether the health authorities thought he could manage or not, and Judith gave Hugh a report on the Winton baby.

As they walked to the car afterwards they were, at least to all outward appearances, in perfect amity with one another.

Just before Judith got out, Hugh said a little curtly: "I've never asked how you found your friend – I'm so sorry. I hope he's getting on all right."

"Oh, yes thanks. He's doing fine now." Judith hesitated and then added boldly: "I've invited him to our house for a week or so when he leaves the hospital. He dreaded having to go to the convalescent home."

Melanie turned round, her face bright with interest. "*He*? Sounds romantic, Judy! Or is it somebody like your father?"

Judith had forgotten that the girl didn't know she had been visiting Sean and she quickly explained.

"Oh, I see." She glanced sideways at her uncle but Hugh kept silent. Nevertheless, Judith fancied that there was disapproval in the line of his jaw.

"I was going to say I'd come and visit him," Melanie went on, "but as he's your boy friend perhaps I'd better not." Her voice was suddenly very sedate. "My uncle didn't like me going out with someone so much older than myself the night he took me to the dance. He said it was very wrong of Sean to ask me."

Memory of the lie she had told flashed into Judith's mind. She longed to rush into Sean's defence to point out that he hadn't known Melanie's real age until afterwards. But what would be the use of stirring it all up again? Hugh would be angry and Melanie would repeat her lie – and be believed – and nothing would be accomplished at all.

She accordingly made no reply, and almost at once the car stopped outside Grove Farm House. Changing into uniform a few minutes later, she reflected with satisfaction that, thanks to getting a lift, she wouldn't be late for surgery after all.

Her father had evidently forgotten that she had expected to be late and made no comment when she arrived punctually. He was looking very pleased about something and immediately told her what it was.

"Andrew Graham was telling me that he's got the report on the tests he carried out on little Kevin Woodward. The child hasn't got leukaemia after all, and we ought to be able to get him right again without too much difficulty."

"I'm so glad!" The reference to leukaemia which had been part of the general gloom so recently, now seemed to Judith to put the finishing touch to a happy afternoon. "He's such a nice little boy," she went on, "that – "

"His niceness has nothing whatever to do with it, Judy," her father reminded her. "It would be just as tragic for him to get leukaemia if he'd been the crossest, most unattractive child in Bedwell Green."

"Yes, of course it would." She accepted the reproof as being well-deserved. "By the way, I saw

Mrs. Winton's baby. He doesn't seem to be progressing very fast."

"I was afraid he'd take his time, but I think he'll make it in the end. He comes of strong healthy farming stock and that must make a difference." He glanced at his watch. "Hadn't we better start surgery?"

They worked steadily, managing to get through a full waiting room in good time, and then relaxed for a few minutes before Rodney started his evening calls.

"I can't make out how people manage to get so many complaints in lovely summer weather," he observed, washing his hands at the basin in a leisurely manner. "I don't usually have more than I had tonight in the worst of the winter."

He let the water out and reached for the towel. "It's funny though, but Hugh was saying only yesterday that there hadn't been so many lately."

Judith turned round and found him looking rather serious. "That was a very meaningful tone, Dad. Or am I imagining things?"

"No, dear, I'm afraid you're not. The fact is that people – *some* people – are boycotting Hugh's surgery, and all because of a few old women who ought to have more sense."

"Because of Melanie, I suppose," Judith said angrily. "It's all so absurd! Melanie's a blood relation; why shouldn't they live at Birch Cottage on their own for a few weeks?"

"No reason at all, but you and I can't influence village opinion like Mrs. Bradbury and her sisters, and even Mrs. Dixon doesn't seem to be entirely approving of the menage."

"I still think they've gone mad. I wouldn't have expected Bedwell Green to be like that. The people all seem so friendly."

"This village is no better and no worse than any other. A few folks haven't got enough to think about and so they fasten on to anything that promises to be even slightly scandalous. They never realise how they hurt people in the process."

"Has Hugh been hurt?" Judith demanded.

"I don't think he realises – yet. But the penny's bound to drop sooner or later."

It dropped the following day, and Judith – to her distress – was involved in it.

The telephone rang just before surgery and when she went to answer it she found that it was Mrs. Jennings, the wife of a smallholder living on the outskirts of Bedwell Market. She had a teenage daughter who was frequently off school with a variety of real and imaginary illnesses.

"Helen's under the weather again," she announced. "Will you ask the doctor to come and see her again, please?"

Behind Judith the door opened and she knew that it was Hugh arriving to take surgery.

"You're on Doctor Renton's list, aren't you?" she asked.

Immediately she sensed that Mrs. Jennings was embarrassed. "Well, I was just going to tell you, Nurse, that I'd rather have one of the others this time – your father for preference."

"Oh! Well, I'll see what I can do." Indignation was blazing in Judith to such an extent that she had difficulty in keeping it out of her voice. If she had been alone, she would have demanded an explanation.

"What seems to be the matter with Helen?" she managed to enquire coolly.

"She's running a slight temperature and complains of pains in her tummy. She's been sick too; otherwise I'd have brought her to the surgery."

Judith promised to ask someone to look in during the day and replaced the receiver.

And inevitably Hugh said: "What was all that about?"

"Just someone wanting a doctor to visit." She scribbled on the pad and hoped he wouldn't ask who it was.

But of course he did, and she was obliged to tell him that it was Helen Jennings who was ill.

"She's one of mine, Judith. I'm starting my round at Bedwell Market today so I can easily call." Hugh sat down at the desk and looked at her in faint bewilderment. "Had you forgotten that the Jennings family are my patients?"

She turned away and busied herself with getting out a clean towel for the washbasin. She would have to tell him – there was no help for it.

"Mrs. Jennings seems to have taken against you for some reason," she said as casually as she could. "She wants one of the others to call."

"I see." Hugh sat in silence for a moment, staring down at his hands folded on the desk top. "No – I'm damned if I do!" He leapt up and took a quick stride across to the window. "I've always got on well with Helen – I like teenagers, as a matter of fact – and with her mother too. Why on earth should they want to be rid of me?"

"I – I can't think of any reason," Judith said unhappily, and not very truthfully.

"Neither can I." He returned to his chair and sat down, immediately brushing back his thick brown hair. "There's something odd going on in this village. I've felt a sort of atmosphere for a week or so."

She looked at him thoughtfully, sharing his distress, and something in her expression made him say reproachfully:

"I believe you *do* know something. If so, I wish you'd let me in on it."

Judith hesitated, decided that he had a right to know, and took the plunge.

"I think it's because of Mrs. Crowfield going away and you and Melanie living at Birch Cottage by yourselves."

"*What?*" Hugh stared up at her in blank amazement. "You have to be joking!"

"Of course I'm not. Some of the older village women are very narrow-minded. I know it's all utterly ridiculous, but I really do think it's at the bottom of all this – this atmosphere."

"Ridiculous? It's an absolute insult! I know I'm not nearly old enough to be Melanie's father, but I *am* her legal guardian."

"Don't let it worry you too much – "

"How can I help it?" he demanded angrily.

"I'm sure it will all die down when Mrs. Crowfield comes back."

He sat brooding for a moment and then asked: "You think I should ignore it then? It would certainly be the most dignified way to handle it."

When Judith had confirmed that this was definitely her opinion, he allowed the subject to drop and made an effort to pull himself together.

But now that his eyes had been opened, he could

not fail to notice the small number of patients who consulted him, and it was in a mood of mingled fury and gloom that he went out to start his round.

As soon as he had driven away, Judith prepared for her geriatric clinic. Normally she enjoyed talking to the old people and found them, in most cases, stimulating and amusing, but today she had difficulty in being her usual friendly self.

As Mrs. Bradbury hobbled in, she longed to give her a piece of her mind on the subject of Dr. Renton and his niece, but she knew it would do no good. The advice she had given Hugh was the right one, she felt convinced, and she must follow it herself if she didn't want to stir up the murky depths of these people's minds and perhaps make matters worse.

But she did relieve her feelings by telling her father all about it at lunchtime, abandoning restraint completely and waxing so indignant about it that Rodney gave her a very searching look.

"You mustn't take it to heart, dear. Hugh's able to look after himself, I'm sure."

"But it's so unfair – "

"Of course it is, but so are lots of other things, and doctors are fair game for the gossipmongers – don't ask me why." He picked up his knife and fork and, with his eyes on his plate, commented quietly: "You seem very interested in Hugh's welfare."

Judith stood poised with a vegetable dish in her hand and two spots of colour burned suddenly in her cheeks.

"He's a colleague of yours. Isn't it natural?"

"Oh yes, but you shouldn't let it worry you as much as you appear to be doing. There's not a word of truth in the old saying 'There's no smoke without fire' and I'm quite sure the whole silly affair will die down very soon."

"I hope you're right." Judith banged the dish down in front of him. "I forgot the beans, but you haven't finished so it's not too late."

She ladled out a generous helping on to his plate and added some to her own. "Changing the subject, I've got something to tell you which didn't seem to get said yesterday. I've invited Sean to stay here while he convalesces. I hope you don't mind."

"Oh – er – not at all." Rodney looked at her in some bewilderment. "Correct me if I'm wrong, but I'd rather got the impression you were no longer interested in Sean."

"I'm sorry for him, that's all."

"D'you think he realises that?"

"I – I hope so." Judith faltered a little. "Honestly, Dad, I'm pretty sure he was only so pleased at the invitation because he didn't want to go to Rowanheath."

But her father did not look particularly convinced and they finished their meal in rather a strained silence.

Washing up afterwards, Judith swished the detergent round with unnecessary vigour and thought how much it resembled the whirlpool of her thoughts at that moment.

Her father's comments had forced her to face up to what had been happening to her these last weeks. She had come home from Cumberton at least half in love with Sean, though she had done her best to put him out of her mind. She was still very fond of him but in an entirely different way.

And the reason?

Judith's personal analysis came to an abrupt halt and her lips twisted into a wry smile. The kitchen sink was no place for romantic dreams; there should be moonlight and the scent of roses, and at her side a tall young man with unruly brown hair and deep-set grey eyes in which she saw the reflection of the yearning in her own heart.

But Hugh never looked at her like that and almost certainly he would never do so. His affection was all centred on the unpredictable teenager in his charge, and apart from her he was interested only in his work.

Judith sighed and tipped out the washing-up water. When she had put everything away neatly she went upstairs to get a room ready for Sean in case he was discharged earlier than expected.

He was installed in it before she even had time to pay him another visit in hospital. The ambulance brought him – much to his annoyance, for he no longer considered himself an invalid – and Judith had difficulty in persuading him that he should be in bed at once.

"I'll be good," he protested. "I won't stir from my chair until you come back from surgery."

"I don't trust you an inch." She looked at his gaunt face and shadowed eyes. "You're not half as strong as you imagine, so go and get into bed *at once.*"

"Only if you'll come and tuck me up."

"I'll pop in as soon as I've changed into uniform."

Ten minutes later she entered his room to find him lying back against his pillows with an air of complete exhaustion.

"You'd better have your supper in bed this evening." She stooped to pick up the clothes he had dropped on the floor and was not surprised to hear a meek agreement.

He was a reasonably good patient for the first two days, and then he began to feel so much better that it was quite a problem to keep him amused.

"Couldn't Melanie come and visit me while you're working?" he suggested hopefully.

Judith looked doubtful. "I could mention it to her if you like, but she might not want to in view of all the fuss there was when you took her to the dance."

"I suppose what you really mean is that her uncle might object," Sean said. "If he does, and if Melanie is half the girl I think she is, then she'll tell him to get lost."

So Judith promised to ring up and find out if Hugh's niece was willing to play the role of sick visitor.

"He isn't really ill now, is he?" Melanie asked quickly. "Because if so – "

"Oh no – he just has to rest a lot and he's getting terribly bored."

"Okay – I'll come then." She was suddenly quite enthusiastic. "I'll bring some records and be along in the morning." On the verge of ringing off her tone changed again. "Don't tell Hugh I'm going to see Sean, please. He might get all steamed up and jealous about it. You'll remember I said I wouldn't visit him at all."

"*Jealous?*" Judith could not keep and amazement out of her voice.

"It was really because he was jealous that he didn't like me going to the dance," Melanie explained. "Hugh's a very possessive type and I adore him for it, but it does make life rather difficult sometimes." A long sigh wafted over the wires to her incredulous listener.

"I'm sure you're exaggerating," Judith said firmly, "but I won't mention it if I can help it. I'll promise you that much."

Coming out of the study, she found that the post had arrived. There were several letters for her father, none for herself, and two for Sean.

One was in his mother's handwriting, which she had already seen, and the other was a neater, more shapely hand which was unfamiliar. Judith glanced at it without curiosity and took them both upstairs.

Sean took them casually and slit open his mother's letter. "I don't know how Mum finds time to write four or five pages but she always does," he commented with a slight air of guilt.

"I don't believe you've written to her once since you came here," Judith accused him.

"I've been too lazy, but I'll do it this morning." He put the other letter down on the bedspread and made no attempt to open it.

"You'll probably have time before Melanie comes. She'll be here later on and she's bringing some records." Judith went across to the door and turned to smile back at him. "It's marvellous to see you looking so much better."

"I feel altogether different, thanks to your good nursing and good food." Sean's voice was unusually serious. "I'll always be grateful to you, Judy, for taking me in like this."

"I'm glad I was in a position to help."

Judith closed the door behind her and hurried downstairs, unhappily aware that she sounded stiff and formal, and almost as middle-aged as Heather invariably did.

Once or twice during the morning she thought of the two who were presumably entertaining themselves at Grove Farm House, and hoped Sean wasn't getting over-tired. Rather to her surprise, when she returned just before lunch, she met Melanie hurrying down the drive.

"I didn't notice the time and I'm late for getting Hugh's lunch. I've just got to get back before he comes or he'll wonder where I've been. See you!" About to race past, she halted suddenly: "Oh, I forgot! Sean asked me to post some letters and I've left them in the hall. Will you do it for me?"

Judith promised that she would and decided to get it off her mind immediately, so that Sean's letter to his mother should be speeded on its way.

She picked up the two envelopes from the hall table and looked at them to make sure that he had indeed written to Mrs. Hargreaves. The top letter was the one she had expected to see and she did not really intend to look at the other one, but somehow it happened.

"Miss Carol Morgan," he had written in his untidy scrawl, and the address was in his home town.

Could this be the answer to the letter which had come only that morning? And who was Carol Morgan?

For a day or two the question nagged at her mind, though she made no attempt to do any probing. And then it was pushed violently into the background by a conversation she had with Mrs. Mayhew, the village woman who helped with the cleaning both at Grove Farm House and Birch Cottage.

CHAPTER ELEVEN

"How MUCH longer's that young chap going to be staying here?" demanded Mrs. Mayhew towards the end of Sean's second week.

Her tone had been most unusually disgruntled and Judith looked at her cleaning woman in dismay.

"He'll be going in a few days, Mrs. Mayhew. I'm very sorry if he's made a lot of extra work for you. I've tried to keep his room as tidy as possible."

"It's not him I mind so much really, miss – it's that girl. When she's been here there's records and empty coke cans and toffee papers all over the place. I have enough to do cleaning up after her at Birch Cottage. Besides –" She broke off and pursed her lips in an uncompromising sort of way.

Here it was again, the same ridiculous prejudice, and in Mrs. Mayhew of all people, whom Judith had hitherto believed to be reasonably broad-minded. But before she could speak, the woman unsealed her lips sufficiently to permit of another comment.

"If I weren't sorry for Mrs. Crowfield being taken advantage of like this, I'd leave – and that's a fact."

"But *why*, Mrs. Mayhew?" The words burst out before Judith could stop them, in spite of her conviction that the gossip was better ignored.

"Because I'm a respectable woman – that's why. And I don't approve of households what isn't."

"You've no right to say that!" Indignation boiled up in Judith so that she no longer cared about discretion, or even the inadvisability of upsetting Mrs. Mayhew.

"No right, haven't I? Just you listen to me, miss –"

"Dr. Renton and Melanie are blood relatives," she went rushing on. "There's no reason in the world why they shouldn't share a house without the need for – for a chaperone."

"Ah!" The woman folded her arms across her apron and looked triumphant. "That's where you're wrong."

"Wrong? What on earth do you mean?"

"They aren't related at all. I had it from the girl's own lips. Dr. Renton's brother and his wife couldn't have any children and they adopted Melanie when she was a few weeks old. And with him being so young and the girl so grown-up like, I think it's downright disgusting them living together all alone at Birch Cottage. And every decent-minded person in the village agrees with me."

All the burning anger which had swept Judith into this horrible conversation with a woman she had always liked, died a sudden death and left her cold with shock.

She said clearly and icily: "I think you mean every narrow-minded old busybody, Mrs. Mayhew. No one who had any real humanity would dream of taking exception to it, specially in view of the terrible tragedy which occurred earlier in the summer. Dr Renton and Melanie *need* each other for – for comfort."

"Narrow-minded old busybody, am I?" Mrs Mayhew could hardly believe her ears. "Well, if that's how you think of me, Miss Lidgate, I'll ask you to accept my notice. I've worked at this house for nearly ten years, first for your Mum and then looking after your father when she died, and I've always done my best to please *you*. But I'll not stay here to be insulted and that's for sure."

"I – I'm sorry. You've always been very good and so reliable," Judith said miserably. "Please, Mrs Mayhew, can't we just agree to differ? I don't know how I'd get on without you."

"No more don't I, *and* you'd not find another woman to do what I've done, not in Bedwell Green you wouldn't."

"Then won't you –"

"No, I won't, and that's a fact. I'm upset, that's what I am and I must say I never thought it'd come to this." And, with an unexpected sniff, she took off her apron and went to put on the shapeless cardigan which she always wore in the summer.

Judith sank down in a chair and put her hands up to her cheeks. They still felt flushed and she realised that the coldness was all inside her.

Why couldn't she have been more tactful? Why did she have to blow her top like that? She could have politely disagreed with Mrs. Mayhew without being downright rude. No wonder the woman had taken offence!

The slam of the back door brought her to her feet but she stifled her instinct to rush in pursuit. Better to leave it for a day or two, and then go round to Mrs. Mayhew's cottage and apologise. Very likely she, too, would have had second thoughts by then. Slightly cheered by this decision, Judith was tempted to sit down again and try to come to grips with the astonishing information which had been given to her. She could still hardly believe that Hugh and Melanie weren't uncle and niece after all.

He thought of her as his niece – she was sure of it.

Or was that only because she wanted to believe it so much?

Shying from the implications of this, Judith looked at the clock and made a real effort to pull herself together. She ought to be getting lunch, not sitting at the table in a dream which threatened to turn into a nightmare.

When she had done the potatoes and put the sausages on the hot plate, she went into the garden to warn Sean that lunch would not be long.

The weather had turned very hot and sultry and the lawn daily grew more yellow. Even the weeds did not grow, which lessened the work considerably, though fallen apples and pears kept Judith busy in other ways.

She found Sean lying in a long chair with his eyes half closed.

"I shall miss all this when I go home on Saturday," he said regretfully.

"You're definitely going then?"

"Afraid so. Mum wants me to spend a week or two with the family before I start work again."

"It's a long drive. Do you feel fit enough, or are you going by train?"

To her surprise he avoided her gaze. "I – er – I'm not sure yet."

"You'd better hurry and make up your mind then," Judith told him lightly.

He made no reply and she returned to the house. As she entered by the french window she noticed that Mrs. Mayhew had left the vacuum cleaner standing in the middle of the floor. The room had a slightly unfinished look, with the furniture not quite in its normal position.

Hastily putting it straight, Judith thought gloomily of the future. However would she find time to do all the housework in addition to her other duties, if the cleaner stuck to her decision not to come again to Grove Farm House?

It was in the front of her mind for the rest of the day, with the result that she forgot the time and was late for evening surgery.

Heather gave her a disapproving look as she entered.

"Dr. Corder's started and he hates being interrupted. It might be a good idea to wait here until he's ready for the next patient."

It was good advice and, though she resented being given it, Judith forced herself to accept it gratefully.

There had been a truce between herself and the secretary since the supper party. Heather seemed to have made a real effort to be friendly and Judith had done her best to reciprocate. Neither of them had been really successful, but at least the atmosphere in the office had been much more pleasant.

Unfortunately, this evening there seemed to be a definite deterioration. Heather, who was looking pale and tired, snapped when Judith asked if she had nearly finished for the day.

"I've got another half-hour's work to do yet. I'm not one of those people who put the cover on the typewriter the minute the clock strikes."

"I'd better keep quiet then, and let you get on with it."

"I'd be grateful if you would."

Annoyed, Judith went into the waiting room, and just then Dr. Corder finished with his first patient and she was able to start work.

"There's a lot of this summer flu about," the elderly doctor observed when, an hour later, they reached the end of the waiting patients. He shot a penetrating look at Judith from beneath his bristling brows. "You're looking a bit peaked yourself, and so's Miss Black. I hope *she's* not getting it."

On any other day Judith would have been slightly amused at the suggestion that, although the practice could do very well without her own services, it could not manage without Heather. But this evening the pointed remark was definitely painful, and she left the surgery feeling even more at odds with the world than before.

In the morning the secretary's chair was empty.

"Where's Heather?" Dr. Graham asked as soon as he arrived. He glanced round the small office in bewilderment, as though suspecting that she might be hiding in a cupboard.

"I'm wondering if she's ill," Judith said. "She didn't look at all well yesterday, but I would have thought she'd let us know."

"She isn't on the phone and that cottage is very isolated." Dr. Graham looked concerned. "I can't ever remember this happening before except when she's on holiday, and the practice just about falls apart then, until she gets back and sorts us all out."

"If we haven't heard anything by the time I've finished my clinic I'll fetch my bike and ride over and see what's wrong."

"Good idea," the doctor approved. "And I'd be very grateful if you'd stop at the village shop on the way and hand in my wife's list of holiday requirements. I was supposed to take it but I didn't have time and my round starts in the opposite direction."

Judith slipped the long list into her pocket and went to fetch the first patient, a ruddy-faced farm worker who had injured his arm in a combine harvester a few days previously.

"It's doing very nicely," Dr. Graham said. "We'll have you back at work in no time."

"Can't I go back tomorrow, doctor? We're that busy trying to finish the harvest before the weather breaks. This hot weather'll end in a thunderstorm, I reckon."

"You won't be fit as soon as that, I'm afraid, Say the day after tomorrow."

As Judith re-bandaged the gash on his arm, she asked the man where he worked.

"Park Farm, Nurse – Mr. Winton's that is."

"That's where Miss Black has her cottage, isn't it? We're worried because she hasn't turned up today."

The man nodded. "She's got that little place about half-a-mile up the track, but I dunno anything about whether she's okay or not. I haven't set eyes on her, not since we were cutting that field that comes up to her garden hedge and she asked us if we were going to burn the stubble. Upset she was, in case the fire should spread to her thatch."

"I can understand that," Judith said. "*Are* you going to burn it?"

"I reckon we will, but there's no call for her to worry. Mr. Winton wouldn't do it unless the wind was right."

Assuming Heather was ill, it wouldn't do her much good to lie in bed thinking about the possibility of fire. More than ever determined to find out what had happened, Judith hurried off to fetch her bicycle as soon as she was free.

She was passing the shop when she remembered Mrs. Graham's order, with the result that she braked sharply and tried to turn round in the road without getting off. An experienced cyclist could have done it easily, but Judith rarely used her bicycle now and she badly misjudged the speed at which she could turn in such a narrow space.

Landing ignominously on her knees in the road, her first thought was for her tights and she was examining them ruefully when she became aware of an approaching car. Her bicycle still lay where it had fallen and she bent to pick it up quickly, knocking her ankle painfully and drawing blood.

The car driver had also braked sharply and he now drew up behind her.

"Have you hurt yourself, Judith?" It was Hugh's voice, and he leapt out and came to her side with every appearance of concern.

"I suddenly remembered I had to call at the shop and I made a mess of turning round." She dabbed at her ankle with a handkerchief and hoped he wouldn't notice the effect his sudden appearance had on her.

"You're bleeding!" He would have stooped to examine her wound if she had not moved her foot sharply.

"It's nothing. I'll see to it when I get home –"

"My dear girl, it ought to be attended to at once."

Judith shook her head. "I haven't got time just now. I'm on my way to Heather's cottage to find out why she didn't come to work this morning. Apparently it's almost unheard of."

"If she's ill she ought to be seen by a doctor,"

Hugh said at once. "I'll drive you up there if you like. It'll be quicker than cycling."

"Would you?" She looked up at him gratefully. "I've rather taken against my bike at the moment. Can you wait a minute while I dash into the shop?"

Having propped her bicycle against a handy wall, Judith hurried into the stores to hand over Mrs. Graham's list. A moment later she joined Hugh in the car.

"I'm a bit vague about where we're going," he admitted as he passed the turning which led to Birch Cottage. "I hope you know."

"I've never been out there but I think I can find it. I was brought up in Bedwell Green, you know, and the neighbourhood is very familiar. If you take the next farm track on the right I think you'll come to the cottage – eventually."

"What a road!" he exclaimed, slowing down to spare the springs of his car.

"I expect it's only used by farm vehicles," Judith said. "Heather doesn't even ride a bike; she always walks to the surgery."

"I wonder if she has any life apart from her work," Hugh said thoughtfully as they bumped along. "She's just as big a mystery to me now as she was when I first joined the practice nearly a year ago. I was quite amazed to find how human she seemed that evening we had supper at your house."

Judith did not answer for a moment, and then she said apologetically: "You'll think I'm awful, but somehow I've never been able to appreciate her properly. She doesn't like me either, though she's tried to hide it lately."

He was so long finding a reply that she ceased to

expect one, assuming that the rutted road needed all his attention. Consequently, when he did answer her, his words seemed all the more astonishing.

"I could never think you 'awful' about anything, Judith. To me you have always seemed to be very good and kind. I've noticed you with the patients when they're nervous – the children specially. You seem to have an instinct for helping people."

He waited for her to speak, but Judith was staring ahead, her eyes fixed on the golden piles of straw bales and her heart thudding in her ears.

"I've always wanted to tell you how much I admired you for giving up your career – and after winning the Gold Medal too – to keep house for your father."

He got his answer then, and the vehemence of it amazed him.

"You're – you're making me sound just like a stuffed dummy in a nurse's uniform!" Judith twisted round in her seat and glared at him. "And I'm not like that! I'm human and full of faults, and I never, never go around shedding sweetness and light in all directions!"

"I never said you weren't human –"

"Well, it sounded like it."

"I must be extremely bad at expressing myself," Hugh said stiffly.

He had been driving more and more slowly and now the car had almost stopped. If they didn't get to Heather's soon, Judith thought wildly, she'd probably burst into tears right there at his side.

When he had tossed his first bouquet into her lap, she had been incredulous, crazily happy, her heart singing like a bird, and then he had spoilt it all, turning what had seemed like something unbelievably wonderful into a repetition of the praise which she had already heard from all sorts of people.

"Do get on a bit quicker," she said sharply. "I've got to get back as soon as possible."

He increased his pace so much that the jolting would have made further conversation almost impossible even if there had been anything to say, and within a few minutes they came in sight of a very small thatched cottage standing beside the track.

"I'll wait here," Hugh said curtly, "until you find out if I'm needed."

A tap on the front door brought no reply and Judith tried the latch cautiously. The door was obviously locked and she went round to the back.

Just above her head there was an open window and a partly drawn curtain blowing in the breeze, and suddenly she heard Heather's voice.

"Who's there?"

"It's me – Judith. We thought you might be ill."

There was the sound of movement and the secretary's face appeared briefly at the window. "I'll come down and let you in."

Heather really did look ghastly, Judith thought as she stepped into the tiny, old-fashioned kitchen. She never had much colour but now her skin matched the cream-coloured wall and she shivered as she pulled a drab blue dressing gown round her.

"I tried to get up this morning but I just couldn't manage it."

"You'd better get right back into bed. It's obvious you're not fit to be standing around."

Judith put out a helping hand as they came to the narrow, almost perpendicular stairs going up behind a door, but Heather ignored it. Somehow she hauled herself up by the handrail and led the way into a pleasant little bedroom with a sloping roof looking out across the cornfields.

"Do you think it's summer flu?" Judith asked.

"I've got a temperature and I feel like death, so I expect it is." Heather subsided thankfully into bed and pulled the blankets up to her chin. "A couple of days' rest will probably put me right."

"I think you ought to see a doctor. As a matter of fact, I've got one outside now –"

"Your father?" Heather's half-closed eyes flew open, but Judith could not be sure whether she welcomed or was horrified at the prospect of a visit from Dr. Lidgate.

"No, it's Hugh Renton. He gave me a lift. Shall I ask him to come in?"

"I suppose you'd better. I shall need a certificate if I'm off work more than three days – not that I intend to be, of course – but perhaps if I have some medicine I shall get better more quickly."

Hugh came quietly upstairs, his professional manner very much in evidence, and gave Heather a thorough examination. When he had finished, his verdict was the one they had been expecting and he went on to insist on at least three days in bed.

"You seem to have picked up a particularly virulent germ and it's affected your chest." He scribbled on a prescription form. "Somebody will bring the cough medicine and tablets later today."

"I'm giving you all so much trouble," Heather said weakly. "I've hardly ever been ill – not once since I came here – and I never thought of the difficulty of getting prescriptions made up."

"You're entitled to live where you like and you've certainly got a very nice little place," Hugh told her. "But I don't think you ought to be left entirely unattended." He looked across at Judith who stood by the window. "Perhaps you could look in tomorrow?"

Just as she was about to mention the district nurse and ask whether it would be in order, Heather broke in emphatically.

"I don't want anybody to come. I'm perfectly capable of lying here alone until I feel better."

"We'll see," Hugh said diplomatically. He opened the door on to the tiny square landing and held it politely for Judith to precede him down the stairs.

They had just reached the kitchen when Heather called after them: "Please lock the door and put the key under the big stone you'll find outside."

"Thank goodness she's making it possible for somebody to get in if necessary." Hugh heaved up the stone and did as requested. "I think she's well aware that she's really quite ill."

Judith hardly noticed his comment. Now that she was alone with him again her thoughts had flown back to the ridiculous way she had behaved on the outward journey. He had exerted himself to pay her a compliment and she had repaid him by completely misunderstanding and losing her temper – for the second time in two days. Why on earth was she so lacking in control?

But, although she knew the answer, she chose to ignore it.

CHAPTER TWELVE

"I've made my arrangements for leaving on Saturday." Sean followed Judith into the kitchen and sat down at the table to watch as she began to make a cake. "I'll probably be off just before lunch."

"By train?" She gave him a keen look and found his expresion unusually enigmatical.

"Er – no." He picked up a knife and began to twirl it round on the table. "And I'm not driving either."

"I was never any good at riddles."

Sean laughed in rather an embarrassed way. "I'll have to come clean, Judy, love – there's no help for it. Somebody's coming to fetch me – an old friend of mine. It's – it's a girl."

"I see." Her lips twitched but she kept her voice serious. "Carol Morgan, by any chance?"

He let the knife fall to the floor with a clatter. "How on earth did you know?"

Judith laughed outright. "I posted a letter for you when Melanie forgot it. It was a long shot really, but I think I'm right, aren't I?"

"Of course you are!" Sean gave a long sigh of relief. "I was dreading telling you – I thought you'd be furious because I'd deceived you."

And she wasn't even indignant, Judith reflected with a faint sense of surprise. Aloud she asked: "Have you known her long?"

"Off and on for years. We were kids together and then I went in for medicine and she trained to be a teacher. No matter how many times we got interested in other people, we always seemed to drift back towards each other. I guess both of us have come to the conclusion that we might as well give in."

"Was Carol around when you went home because your father was ill?"

Sean nodded, his shamefaced look returning. "That was when I began to think seriously about her."

"So that was why I didn't hear anything from you." Judith began to beat eggs with great vigour. "And yet you came back here and tried to continue with me?"

"Well – I'm very fond of you, Judy –"

"And Carol was a long way away," she interrupted, a shade of bitterness in her voice. "I hope she realises what she's taking on."

"I reckon she knows me pretty well by now."

"And loves you in spite of it?" Judith smiled and, acting on impulse, came over to him and kissed him. "There's no accounting for tastes!"

"No hard feelings?" Sean asked, clutching her arm when she would have moved away.

"None at all. I'm very glad."

She was so obviously sincere that he relaxed and started to talk quite naturally about Carol. By the sound of it she was a girl with a strong personality, and Judith began to look forward to meeting her.

When the baking was finished, they spent a lazy afternoon in the garden before she had to get ready for work.

As she crossed the Green, she saw her father's car draw up outside the surgery and he waited for her to join him before going in.

"We've arranged for Heather to get her medicine," he told her. "Mr Winton called in at the dispensary to pick up some tablets for his wife – I expect you knew she was home from hospital – and he said he'd take it. He's going to leave it outside the door and call up to Heather to tell her it's there."

They passed through the office, which seemed strangely empty, and Rodney glanced at the covered typewriter.

"I've never known Heather absent before, or not from illness anyway. The place doesn't seem the same without her."

"I expect she'll soon be back," Judith said.

"Oh yes, but I'm a bit worried in case she doesn't wait until she's really fit." He hesitated, absent-mindedly jingling the money in his pocket. "Hugh says he suggested you should call and it wasn't well received, but I think you should ignore that. You could go along this afternoon, couldn't you?"

Judith hesitated. "I *could*, but –"

"Then I hope you will," Rodney finished firmly.

It practically amounted to an order, and he was her boss as well as her father, so Judith subdued her reluctance to visit the cottage again and set out on her bicycle later on that day, grimly determined to do her best for Heather whether the visit was well received or not.

The rutted track was a severe test of her riding skill but she managed to stay on and eventually arrived in safety.

Should she unlock the door and go in, or shout up to the window first?

Deciding on compromise, she uncovered the key

and opened the door before calling out, thus giving Heather no time to forbid her to enter.

The kitchen, which had previously looked so clean and neat, had already acquired a shut-up smell; there was an unwashed cup and saucer on the draining board, and on the window sill a plant drooped in need of water.

Judith attended to it first and then began to climb the ladderlike stairs, calling out again as she did so but receiving no audible reply.

The bedroom door was closed and she opened it after a quick tap. "I came to see if there was anything I could do –"

The words died on her lips as the invalid, who seemed to have been dozing, interrupted angrily.

"I *told* you I didn't need anybody!"

"I'm not sure you're the best judge of that at the moment," Judith said calmly, looking at the tumbled bed. "Have you taken your temperature today?"

"No, I haven't – and I don't want it taken either." The words ended in an outburst of coughing.

"I don't expect you felt like bothering, but it really ought to be done." Judith deftly inserted the thermometer.

Noting the over-bright eyes and feverish glow of the normally pale skin, she was not surprised to find that the mercury had risen rather alarmingly.

"I hope you've been taking your tablets," she said.

"There hasn't been time for more than three lots. But I had a dose of cough mixture in the night."

"How are you sleeping?"

"Badly."

"There's probably a sedative in the mixture – that

should help by the time you've had a few more doses. Be careful not to take it too often though, won't you?"

"You're only a nurse," Heather sneered, "so it's no good handing out advice and expecting me to follow it as though you were a doctor."

Judith ignored the comment, knowing it to be prompted by the abnormal state of mind caused by a high temperature. "Do you feel up to sitting in a chair while I make the bed?" she asked.

"I'll manage." Refusing a helping hand, she struggled to her feet and almost collapsed onto the chair which Judith had put ready.

She watched in morose silence as the bed was remade and then staggered back into it with a sigh of relief.

"I'm sure you must be much more comfortable now," Judith said. "Is there anything else you'd like me to do before I go?"

She had not expected thanks but she was completely taken aback by the venom in the reply she received.

"I'd rather be miserably uncomfortable than have *you* to put things right for me!"

Indignant, and more than a little hurt, she stared back at her patient. It would be easier to say nothing – she knew that perfectly well – and yet she could not resist taking Heather up on it.

"I'm sorry you feel like that about me. I know you don't like me but I don't see any reason for talking as though – as though you *hated* me."

"Don't you?" The hard, glittering stare turned in her direction and she almost quailed before the intensity of Heather's dislike. "I can soon tell you.

"You threw up your hospital work, didn't you, and came home to keep house for your father – you, a gold medallist! It didn't mean anything to you that you wrecked my life; in fact, you were probably so busy being the self-sacrificing devoted daughter that you didn't even notice –" She broke off to cough.

"How could I notice?" Judith stood at bay and struggled to defend herself. "*You* certainly wouldn't want me to, not when you're in a – a normal state, and in any case I haven't the faintest idea what you're talking about."

Heather raised herself on one elbow and began to speak more rationally. "I'll tell you. Your father would have married me if you hadn't appointed yourself his housekeeper. He was growing fond of me – he made it quite plain – and I –" Her voice trembled and broke. "I've always loved him, right from the time I first came as his secretary, before the group practice was started. Your mother guessed, I think, but she was a sweet person and always kind to me."

"I'm glad you approved of *her* anyway," Judith said bitterly.

"She was different from you. *She* would never have flaunted youth in my face, the way you've done."

"Well, of course she wouldn't! She was several years older than you."

"You know what I mean. You've pretended to be friendly but all the time you were only patronising me – Heather Black, plain, dowdy, spinsterish –"

"You don't have to be that way. Why don't you try making the best of yourself, for heaven's sake?"

Judith stopped, appalled. She must be out of her mind letting Heather get under her skin like this. The poor creature hardly knew what she was saying, and even if she meant every word of it, she would never, never have given voice to it if she hadn't been ill.

"I think you've talked quite enough."

There was authority in her voice and Heather seemed to recognise it, or perhaps she was so exhausted by her tirade that she was glad to stop. Whatever the reason, she lay back against her pillows, breathing rather fast, and closed her eyes.

"You'll probably be so much better tomorrow that you won't need a visit from anyone." Judith moved over to the door and glanced round the room to see if she had forgotten anything.

"I certainly don't want one from you – or that Dr. Renton either."

"What on earth's made you take against him?" Judith asked incautiously, forgetting that she had told Heather to stop talking. "He can't possibly have interfered in your life the way you say I have."

"No, of course not, but he's a disgrace in my opinion, living there with that girl who's not his niece."

Had *everybody* known about it except herself? Judith wondered drearily.

Aloud, she said firmly: "Dr. Renton's private life is his own affair, and I think it's disgusting that people should talk such nonsense about him and Melanie."

It was obvious that Heather would have continued the argument, but a paroxysm of coughing prevented it, and Judith was able to escape.

She went slowly and sadly down the stairs, convinced that she had done more harm than good by coming. She had probably sent the patient's temperature soaring up even further, and she had certainly left her in a far from peaceful frame of mind which would not be at all conducive to the sleep she badly needed.

Mounting her bicycle uncertainly on the track, she found questions pounding at the gates of her mind, questions for which she scarcely dared to find an answer.

Did her father resent her presence in his house? Had he all the time been wishing she had stayed at St. Helen's and, because of his affection for her, been unable to confess it? It was bitterly painful to realise that her return might – just possibly *might* – have been as unwelcome as Heather had said it was.

And what was she to do now? It would be impossible for her to broach the subject, and even if she did she would be unlikely to learn the truth.

As for Heather, the best that could be hoped for her was that she would recover from her illness with only a vague memory of the terrible things she had said and the way she had bared her secret soul.

At lunch, Judith found herself watching her father keenly when he asked after the secretary's welfare, but she learnt nothing from her examination.

"She certainly seems to have a bad dose of flu," she told him cautiously, "and I suppose it will have to run its course. Er – she wasn't very pleased at my visit; I think she wants to be left alone to get over it in her own way."

He nodded, obviously not surprised. "Heather's very independent. Perhaps we ought to respect her wishes. I suggest we leave her until the weekend and then look in. She might even be up and about." He switched his attention to Sean and began to talk about his impending departure.

Only two more days and their guest would be gone. Judith did not know whether to be pleased or sorry, but one thing she was quite certain about. This time it would be for good; there must be no more dividing of his favours.

"You'll have something to eat before you go, won't you?" she said on Saturday morning. "I want to meet Carol properly. 'Hullo' and 'goodbye' won't tell me anything about her."

He grinned and suggested cheekily: "Why not ask Melanie too? Then I'd have three girl friends sitting at the same table!"

"Oh, I don't think –"

"Please, Judy – it's my last wish and you can't refuse it. Melanie's been a great kid keeping me amused all this week, and I think she's earned a lunch."

So Judith could only smile and give in, but it turned out to be an odd sort of luncheon party. Her father was delayed and did not appear at all, and Carol Morgan seemed unexpectedly shy.

She was an attractive girl, with hair as dark as Judith's but worn much longer, and she had the brown eyes which went with it and a bright colour. A very determined chin and a firm mouth showed that she would probably be able to handle Sean.

Melanie was as self-possessed as ever and helped considerably to keep the conversation going. Afterwards she stood by Judith's side to say goodbye and Sean kissed them both while Carol busied herself with stowing odds and ends in her mini.

"I'll always remember – everything," he said in a low voice in Judith's ear.

Knowing that he would inevitably soon forget, she was nonetheless touched by his words.

"Take care, Sean dear, and do be careful not to overdo it." She returned his kiss with affection and waved as they drove away.

"I like Sean but he's terribly *young*, don't you think?" Melanie said thoughtfully.

"He's a lot older than you – nearly as old as – as your uncle."

"I meant mentally. I don't think years have much to do with a person's age. That's why Hugh and I get on so well together."

"Which reminds me," Judith said deliberately. "I heard the other day that you aren't really his niece at all, that your parents adopted you. It's funny you never mentioned it."

"Is it?" Melanie sounded genuinely surprised. "I suppose it just never cropped up. Mummy and Daddy couldn't have any children and so they adopted me when I was just five weeks old."

So it really was true. Not until then had Judith realised quite how much she had hoped it might not be.

"I shall be fifteen on September the third," Melanie continued. "So I've only got one more year at school before I can leave. I don't want to go back at all really – I seem to have grown right away from school these last few weeks – but I know I've got to."

"I expect the time will soon pass. What do you want to do when you leave?"

Judith had asked the question idly and felt little interest in the answer, but a strange expression flitted across Melanie's face as she apparently debated what she should say.

"I'm not very attracted towards having a career, and Daddy left me some money so I don't need to earn very much." She hesitated and glanced at Judith from beneath her lashes. "Shall I tell you a secret?"

"If – if you like."

"Hugh and I have become so fond of each other that we want to marry as soon as I'm old enough – perhaps in two or three years' time. He's twelve years older than me, but that's nothing really – specially when it's the man who's the older one. Lots of very successful marriages have had that sort of difference between husband and wife."

Tall and slender, enchantingly pretty, she smiled down at Judith with all the assurance in the world. Then, with a nonchalant wave of her hand, she sauntered away in the direction of Birch Cottage.

CHAPTER THIRTEEN

It was oppressively hot, and Melanie walked more and more slowly. The grass of the Green was dry and yellowish, and the pond level had sunk by several inches. Not very far away a pall of black smoke showed where either straw or stubble was being burned, and an almost imperceptible movement of air was bringing the acrid smell to the village.

Melanie sniffed it like a dog scenting game, and wondered whether it would be possible to go and have a look. Fire had always fascinated her; she was was both attracted and terrified by it.

As she hesitated at the top of Church Lane, she remembered that Hugh had said that he would be at home during the afternoon and he had reminded her that Mrs. Crowfield returned that evening.

"We ought to do some tidying up before she gets here. The kitchen, you must admit, is in a bit of a mess."

"Mrs. Mayhew did it on Thursday," Melanie protested.

"Yes, love, but you've served up several meals since then and you aren't the world's most methodical cook."

"Okay – anything you say," she agreed amiably.

Glancing at her face, Hugh congratulated himself on the change in her. She had lost that pinched look she had when she came, the dark shadows had vanished from beneath her eyes and she had acquired a healthy tan.

No doubt she still mourned her parents sincerely, but she had recovered from the first shock and time would eventually heal the wound which lay deeper. This quiet time at Bedwell Green had been just what she needed.

When she came in after her lunch at Grove Farm House, he was just finishing a snack of bread and cheese and he greeted her with an approving smile.

"Good girl – I thought you might be persuaded to spend the afternoon with Judith."

"I don't think she wanted me. She seemed a bit depressed, I thought. I expect it's because of losing Sean to that other girl."

There was a pause and then Hugh said grimly: "*He's* no loss! Do you really think she minded?"

"Oh yes, I'm sure she must have. He's been her boy friend for a long time. I say, Hugh, there's a fire over there somewhere –" she waved a hand vaguely "– behind the church –"

"Yes, I know. They're burning the stubble at Park Farm, but if you're thinking of going to have a look, may I remind you that there's work to be done."

"I wouldn't want to go by myself. Could you take me later on?"

"It will all be over by the time we've finished here." He stood up and carried his plate to the draining board. "I'm going to clean the sink for a start and you'd better put those groceries away."

They worked amicably for some time, with Hugh doing the larger share of the chores, and then stopped for a cup of tea.

"Have you got to go out now?" Melanie asked.

"I've got some evening calls to make."

She jumped up and came round the table to perch

on it close to his side. "Take me with you – please! I've been so good doing all this horrible tidying up – I'm sure I deserve a break. Besides, I don't want to be here all alone when Mrs. Crowfield arrives; she's so schoolmarmy and I can never think of anything to say to her."

He smiled. "I didn't think you were ever hard up for words! Do you really want to come all that much?"

"Yes, I do – honestly."

"Very well – just this once, but leave the transistor behind. I've got to go to the other side of Bedwell Market and we might treat ourselves to a meal on the way back There's a good place there."

"Super!" Melanie flung her arms round his neck and kissed him. "Can we stop and look at the fire on the way?"

He shook his head. "I've already told you there'll be nothing to see by now."

But he was wrong about that.

As they got into the car he was reminded of Heather. The smoke wouldn't have done her chest any good and would certainly have made her cough, particularly if Mr. Winton happened to have been burning the field next to her cottage.

Perhaps he ought to drive up the track and see how she was?

At this point it occurred to him that Judith might already have paid another visit; it had been left a bit uncertain as to whether she would go or not. He felt annoyed with himself because he had not remembered to check on it.

"I've just thought of a phone call I ought to make," he said abruptly to Melanie. "It won't take a minute."

Back at the house he dialled the Lidgate number, only to hear the voice of the operator telling him to ring Dr. Corder instead, which would have been no use to him at all. Judith and her father must both be out.

He had in actual fact only missed them by about ten minutes. Judith had been at home all the afternoon, lying on her bed with her face in the pillow. From time to time she would struggle for control, and then once more be overwhelmed by misery.

She hadn't cried like this since her mother died, nor felt so desolate either. She and her father had comforted each other then, both of them striving for composure so as not to upset the other too much. They had battled through it together and attained a certain measure of acceptance.

But now she was entirely alone, and her beloved father was part of her misery, a traitor – so it seemed to her in her grief – to her mother's memory.

Unless Heather had been lying, but that Judith couldn't believe. She might have been exaggerating, perhaps indulging in wishful thinking, but not making it all up. There must have been *some* foundation for her assertion that Rodney would have married her if his daughter hadn't come home.

The inference that he hadn't wanted Judith home, that she had spoiled all his plans, was desperately painful. But she had managed to live with the suggestion for two days without breaking down.

It wasn't Heather's bitter, dagger-sharp words which were causing the greatest distress now – much as she hated to remember them. It was Melanie's confidence regarding what she called her "secret"

– the possibility of a marriage between herself and Hugh.

For Judith, too, had a secret which had lain hidden in her heart for she scarcely knew how long. At first she had been quite unaware of it, and even when she began to suspect its existence she had refused to face up to it.

But her love for Hugh had grown so quietly and gently that it had been easy for her to ignore it. Until today. She was aware of it now all right, but the knowledge brought her no happiness, nothing but the blackest despair.

Judith sat up and pressed her hands over her aching eyes. The lids felt burning hot and swollen – she must look a terrible sight, and her father had said he would be home about five o'clock. She couldn't remain hidden in her room much longer.

Cold water splashed on her face and a quick, cool shower helped a lot. She felt utterly exhausted, her head stuffed with cotton wool and her throat strained with sobbing, but at least she didn't look too bad.

She had just made some tea when Rodney came in and accepted a cup gratefully.

"It's sweltering today!" He mopped his face and changed the subject abruptly. "I keep wondering how Heather is."

His concern was another stab wound but Judith hid it courageously. "She's probably up by now and feeling quite different."

"And she might be a lot worse. We agreed to leave her until the weekend, which means today." He glanced at the clock. "Let's both go along and see how she is."

Frantically Judith struggled to think of some

excuse for refusing. She didn't want to go near the cottage ever again, and to visit it in her father's company would be an agony.

But no inspiration came, and a few minutes later she found herself sitting, silent and rigid with nerves, in his car and being driven through the village towards Park Farm.

Just as they passed the turning to the church, Rodney said sharply: "What's all that smoke?"

"Burning stubble, I expect," Judith suggested without much interest.

"They were doing that earlier. I remember thinking it would be very unpleasant for Heather. But this is fresh smoke – I'm sure of it – and it's from the same direction, which must mean the fire's broken out again." He pressed his foot down on the accelerator and the car leapt forward.

They came to the track and turned up it, bumping and skidding over the ruts, and travelling much faster than Rodney would have dreamt of doing under normal circumstances. Judith, held in place by her seat belt, had her breath almost jolted out of her body as they lurched along.

"It looks terribly near the cottage," she said anxiously, all her personal problems temporarily forgotten.

But it was impossible to get a clear view on account of the hedges and they both knew they would have to wait until they were almost there before their fears would be allayed – or confirmed.

"I'm thinking of that thatched roof," Rodney muttered. "In this dry weather, it would only need a spark –"

He turned the last corner and the cottage stood

before them, and both of them immediately exclaimed in horror.

The thatch was already burning fiercely.

The car skidded to a halt and they ran the last twenty yards, their nostrils full of the smell of smoke and their minds asking the same question.

Why was there no sign of life? Heather – no matter how ill she might feel – should have been outside by now, rescuing valuables, perhaps even dragging out furniture; danger often gave people incredible strength. But to all appearances she either wasn't there, or she was still in bed.

Winning the race by a few yards, Judith sped round to the back door, hoping to find it open. But it was closed and locked, and looked exactly as she had left it on Thursday.

"The key!" Ignoring the hot breath of the burning garden hedge, she flung herself at the stone and turned it over.

"It's not there!" Alarmed, she stared up at her father. "Perhaps Heather felt better and went out." She broke off to cough as smoke eddied towards them.

"We've got to check." Rodney stared round distractedly. "We'll have to break a window."

"Let's try shouting first, Dad. The bedroom's only just above our heads. If Heather's there and she's locked the door for some reason – perhaps so nobody would disturb her again – she surely *must* hear us."

They both called out Heather's name as loudly as they could, stopping every few seconds to listen, but they heard nothing.

"I can't understand why nobody from the farm has turned up," Rodney said. "Surely they must have noticed the smoke by now and sent for the fire engine."

"It would have to come from Cumberton –"

"Yes, of course." He snatched up the stone which should have concealed the back door key. "I'm not waiting any longer. Stand back, Judy."

As the glass of the kitchen window shattered and fell noisily to the concrete below, another car stopped just down the track and Hugh, followed by Melanie, came leaping to join them.

"We saw the smoke from the road," he panted. "Can't you make her hear?"

"I'm going to climb in the window and find out," Judith put in.

"You might cut yourself on the bits of glass. Much better let me try," Hugh said at once.

"Have you seen the size of the window?" A faint smile flickered across her face. "You'd almost certainly get stuck, and what good would that do?"

"I'll give you a lift up, then."

She felt herself seized in strong arms, and in the midst of her fear of the fire and concern for Heather every sense was aware of the sweetness of the momentary contact with him.

And then she was half way through the window, vaguely conscious of blood running down her bare arm, and scrabbling wildly with her toes against the the wall as she searched for something to cling to.

The kitchen tap provided her with a solid object to grip, and after that it was easy. Steadied by Hugh in the background, she drew the lower half of her body through the aperture and landed in a heap on the floor.

About to race for the stairs, she remembered that

she had to unlock the door first and let the men in.

But the key wasn't there, which made it almost certain that Heather had recovered and gone out, taking it with her.

Her father's anxious face was looking in at her and she hastily explained the position.

"I'll just dash upstairs and check, Dad. I won't be a minute."

"Do be careful, dear." He glanced upwards in alarm as the fire roared more loudly. "That roof may cave in at any moment –"

Heedless of his warning, Judith was already on her way. At the top of the stairs she paused to get her breath as smoke swirled around her. The bedroom door was open but she could scarcely see across the room and the bed was only faintly visible.

Surely it was occupied? Judith rubbed her eyes and took a step forward, and at that moment the breeze which was fanning the flames above drove the smoke away from her and she saw Heather lying there, apparently asleep and oblivious alike of the fire and the shouting.

Her heart missed a beat. This was no ordinary sleep. She must either be drugged or . . .

Terrified, Judith leapt across to the bed and seized the limp wrist. There was no time to search for a pulse, but it was warm and that was enough.

"Heather! Wake up! Your house is on fire." Judith dragged the inert figure upright and shook it frantically.

The lashes quivered and she half opened her eyes, but the effort of keeping them open seemed too great and she relapsed into slumber.

She must have taken something – perhaps too many doses of the cough mixture and rather a lot of aspirin. Whatever the cause of her near-coma, it would be impossible to get her to move under her own steam.

There was shouting going on outside and Judith sped to the window. Instead of the three faces she had expected to see, there were now half-a-dozen. Mr. Winton had come at last and two of his men.

"For God's sake, be quick, Judith!" That was Hugh's voice full of anguish.

Her father was calling out too but she cut in on him. "Heather's here, but I can't move her. She seems to be drugged." Her mind racing at frantic speed, she went rushing on: "I'll come down and let you in – by the front door."

Mr. Winton was shouting something about the fire engine being on its way, but she scarcely noticed. She was downstairs without being aware that she had moved and struggling with the bolts on the rarely used front door.

It was open at last and Rodney and Hugh burst in.

"Get outside at once, Judith," her father ordered her. "There's no time to lose."

They pounded past her towards the stairs and she watched them go in bleak despair. They were the two people she loved best in the world and they were heading straight into the most terrible danger.

If only she could have gone with them . . . But she had sense enough to know that she would only be in the way. There wouldn't really be room for both of them on that horrible staircase and the limp body of Heather as well. Speed would be impossible, and yet it was speed which was most desperately needed.

Melanie appeared suddenly in the open doorway. "Where's Hugh? Has he gone upstairs?" She flung herself across the sitting room, screaming at the top of her voice. "Hugh! Don't go up there – you'll get caught by the fire –"

Judith plunged after her and seized her arm. "It's no good trying to stop him. He's – he's got to do what he can. Come outside with me."

"I won't – I won't!" She began to struggle desperately.

Exerting all her strength, Judith dragged her towards the open air. "Don't be daft, Melanie. Hugh will be all right –" Oh God, let it be true! "They couldn't just let Heather lie there and do nothing."

"I don't care what happens to her – I don't care."

Understanding her distress and sharing it, Judith merely tightened her grip, and Melanie suddenly crumpled into tears and made no further resistance. Outside, they stood close together – united in their pain, though only one of them was aware of it – and gazed upwards.

The thatch above the bedroom had now burnt right through and was attacking the rafters. Long greedy tongues of flame licked at the dry old wood and soon had it blazing. From an open window came a great billowing cloud of smoke and it was horribly tinged with red.

"I can't bear to look!" Melanie put both hands over her face and her slender body shook with sobs.

But Judith stood there, frozen in spite of the heat, and like the three men still stared silently at what remained of the roof, in her heart a desperate prayer that it might hold out a few moments longer.

But, just as they heard the siren of the fire engine in the distance, the last fragments of timber and thatch fell in and the bedroom curtains disappeared in a sheet of flame.

CHAPTER FOURTEEN

IT SEEMED to Judith that she had been sitting on a chair in the casualty department at St. Helen's Hospital ever since she could remember. All that happened before – the fire, the discovery of Heather helpless in bed, her father and Hugh racing upstairs to save her – seemed like something she had dreamt long, long ago.

But it wasn't long ago; it was only a couple of hours, if her watch was to be believed.

At her side Melanie stirred. "Do they *have* to take all this time?"

"They've got to be careful. When there are – are several different injuries to deal with, it's easy to miss something."

Across the wide reception hall curtain rings rattled and both girls turned their heads sharply. Rodney Lidgate, one wrist bandaged and with a curious lop-sided look caused by losing some of his hair on one side and also one eyebrow, emerged from a cubicle and came walking briskly towards them.

Judith sprang to her feet. "How do you feel, Dad? Are they letting you go home?"

"I'd like to see them try to keep me in!" He smiled wryly. "There's nothing wrong with me that can't be put right quite quickly."

"They've taken Heather to women's medical," Judith told him. "She's got a bit of congestion, due to the smoke and also the flu, and they want her to get fully over the effects of taking too much dope."

"I'm glad she's going to be properly looked after." He struggled for composure. "What on earth did she do it for, Judy? I've asked and asked myself *why* – "

"I talked to her while she was waiting to be looked at, but she insisted it was only because she was fed up with not sleeping and she wanted to be left in peace. That was why she fetched the key from outside and locked the door. She thinks she must have taken the key upstairs with her, but she can't really remember."

"I suppose we'll have to accept that," Rodney said unhappily.

"I think it's the truth, Dad. Heather didn't take a real overdose; she only made herself abnormally sleepy, for what seemed to her very good reasons."

Behind them Melanie spoke suddenly. "I don't know why you have to go on about Heather when we still don't know what's happening to Hugh."

"I shouldn't think they'll be much longer," Rodney assured her. "He's in good hands. It's lucky that Mr. Ferguson was on the premises – he's an excellent chap for head injuries."

"Will he have to operate?" Melanie said dolefully.

"We can't possibly guess the answer to that, but you mustn't worry. Hugh will be all right."

"But you don't *know* that – you're just saying it to cheer me up." She shuddered and looked about her with distaste. "How I hate hospitals! That awful smell makes me feel sick."

Father and daughter both looked at her pityingly. It was strange, Judith reflected, how all personal emotions seemed to be submerged when something like this happened. She was no longer jealous of either Heather or Melanie – and she had been, she freely admitted it now; all that really mattered at that moment was that Hugh should recover from the injuries he had received when the roof collapsed.

He had been at the top of the stairs, her father had explained to her in the ambulance, and his body had sheltered Heather's limp form from the burning timbers. Rodney's own burns were quite superficial, and his sprained wrist had been acquired when he slipped on the stairs and put all his weight on it. It was not until the firemen had come rushing in and rescued them all that he had even noticed it.

Hugh had been carried out unconscious, his head and shoulders blackened by the fire. The question to which they were all awaiting an answer was whether he had received a fractured skull.

Rodney joined the two girls on the row of chairs, but almost immediately he got up again.

"I think I'll go upstairs to the ward and see how Heather is." His eyes met Judith's and quickly looked away.

She got up and walked with him to the door, her tired mind searching for something to say which would show him she understood. Eventually she decided to come right out with it.

"I know how you feel about Heather, Dad – that you've grown to – to love her, and you mustn't think I shall mind if you want to marry her."

He turned to her in astonishment. "How could you possibly know? I was terribly careful, and so afraid of hurting you. I felt sure you'd resent the mere suggestion that I might put someone in your mother's place."

"Why shouldn't you marry again?" He mustn't

guess that her first reaction had been exactly as he had feared. "You're still under fifty, and Heather would be – very suitable."

"Yes, she would," Rodney said eagerly, "and we get on so well together. That rather offhand manner of hers hides a very warm, sympathetic nature. We have similar tastes too, and she'd never mind how much I talked about my work. The only snag is – "

"Me."

In spite of her efforts, Judith's tone had been bleak, and her father went on a little reproachfully:

"I was only going to say that you've given up a great deal to come home and keep house for me, and I feel very guilty because I was too much of a coward to tell you about Heather before it was all arranged."

"It shouldn't be too difficult to undo it all," Judith said thoughtfully. "After all, I did win the Gold Medal and that ought to count for something. As soon as we get back to normal after today I'll go along to St. Helen's and see if they can find me a job."

"You're a great girl." Rodney's voice was husky. "And please don't feel you've got to be in a hurry about it. Grove Farm House will always be your home – you know that."

She smiled up at him as he went through the swing doors and did not answer. But on the way back to Melanie she made a resolution to snatch at the first opportunity of getting away from Bedwell Green. She had loved the village once – and would do so again, she hoped – but at the moment the whole place had gone sour on her.

A white-coated doctor had appeared and Judith

quickened her pace. There must be news of Hugh – at last.

"I'm glad to tell you that there's no fracture at all, and the burns are only second degree. Dr. Renton will have to spend a few days in hospital, of course – perhaps even a week, but – "

Melanie gave a little skip of happiness. "What a relief! I couldn't bear to think that you might have to operate on his head, and with the skin all burnt too."

Judith said nothing. Her heart was too full for words, and she could only offer up a silent prayer of gratitude.

"Can I see him?" Melanie was begging.

"Not tonight. There'd be no point in it because he's heavily sedated. Come tomorrow afternoon and he'll probably be feeling a lot better."

"I'll do that." She smiled at him prettily. "And thank you very much, doctor, for all you've done."

But when he had left them and she turned back to Judith her eyes looked enormous in a white, strained face. "Can't we go home now, Judy? I'm so tired."

"As soon as my father comes back. I suppose we'll have to get a taxi." She hesitated and then forced herself to go on. "Would you like to come and stay at our house? You'll be lonely at Birch Cottage without – without Hugh."

"Oh, thank you – I'd be very glad. I don't like Mrs. Crowfield very much, and she's back from her holiday now."

"She'll wonder where you both are. We'll have to ring up as soon as we get home."

There was so much to do – phone calls to be made and a bed to be got ready and unwanted food provided – that by the time Judith reached her own bed she was so weary that she fell instantly asleep.

No one had remembered that the following day was Sunday and there was no bus into Cumberton, so Melanie had to content herself with ringing up the hospital.

"All they'd say was that Hugh's condition was satisfactory," she grumbled. "And that doesn't tell you *anything*."

Judith spent the day in a sort of trance though she tried to help her father work out a temporary reorganisation of the practice. With Dr. Graham on holiday and Hugh in hospital, it was going to be very difficult to ensure that no patients were neglected.

On Monday she had a pleasant surprise. Mrs. Mayhew came back.

"I do feel I was a bit hasty-like, miss, and I reckon you could do with some help, what with your poor father's sprained wrist and that girl being here and all." Whipping off her cardigan, she prepared for work. "Just fancy Dr. Renton being such a hero! It makes you think, doesn't it?"

Judith agreed that it did, though she was not sure exactly what she was supposed to be thinking – except that village opinions could change remarkably quickly and Hugh's heroism had apparently triumphed over his lack of morals.

"It's very sad for Miss Black losing her little house," Mrs. Mayhew went on, "though they do say it can be repaired, and in the meantime Mrs. Winton has asked her to stay at the farmhouse. It's only right, if you ask me, them being responsible. Not that it was exactly Mr. Winton's fault. He told one of his men to make quite sure the fire was out before he left it and the young chap had a date with his girl and so he was a bit careless." She shook her head lugubriously. "You can't be too careful with fire and that's a fact."

"I should have thought Mr. Winton might have seen to it himself," Judith said.

"But he had to drive his wife to fetch the baby back from the hospital, didn't he? It was a great day for them, with the child doing all right at last, and then when they got back they saw the fire. A shocking sight it must have been – shocking!"

Judith did not want to be reminded of the fire. She had dreamt about it last night, and had awakened shaking with fear and with Hugh's name on her lips.

Desperately she longed to see him and discover for herself the extent of his injuries. But it was Melanie who had that privilege and she went off on the bus that afternoon, carrying a big bunch of flowers from the garden at Grove Farm House.

The report she brought back with her was alarming.

"I can hardly bear to look at him, Judy. His head is all bandaged but they've left his face uncovered, and it's all horrible blisters. He doesn't look like Hugh at all."

"Does he *seem* like Hugh?"

"I suppose so," Melanie said reluctantly, "in a way, but he doesn't want to talk much."

"I expect he has concussion, which means that he ought to keep very quiet."

"Perhaps I'd better take a book with me next time and just sit and read," Melanie suggested with unusual sarcasm.

She went regularly to Cumberton for three days and then announced that she had a headache and didn't feel well enough to go.

"That funny smell which hangs about the hospital is sure to make it worse." She hesitated and then added honestly: "And I do really hate seeing Hugh looking so awful."

"He'll miss you," Judith pointed out sharply.

"Couldn't you go instead of me? Then I can sit in the garden in the shade until I feel better."

Judith caught her breath. She had watched Melanie leave to catch the bus every afternoon with bitter envy eating its way like acid into her heart. She had forced herself to come to terms with her father's love for Heather, but the thought that Hugh might one day marry Melanie was like a deep suppurating wound which was poisoning her whole being.

"Very well." She was deliberately casual. "I want to visit St. Helen's for another purpose altogether, and I can easily fit in a visit to Hugh."

It would have been sensible, she knew, to seek out one of the nursing officers first and find out if there were any prospects of work for her, or possibly make an appointment for later during the afternoon.

But once she had reached the hsopital her one thought was to see Hugh. Her cheeks were burning and her hands like ice as she tapped on his door. She was trembling as she opened it in response to his "Come in" and her breathing was as rapid as though she had run all the way up the stairs.

As soon as she saw him she realised how Melanie must have felt. He was leaning back against a great heap of pillows, his hands lying idle on the bedspread. Dark glasses covered his eyes and contrasted in a dramatic way with the whiteness of his bandages and the red blistered skin on his cheeks.

"Oh, Hugh!" Without any conventional greeting, Judith crossed swiftly to the bed. "Your eyes – are they all right?"

It was impossible to tell from his face whether he was surprised to see her, but his voice hadn't altered and in it she detected astonishment and also another emotion which she hardly dared to call gladness.

"There's nothing wrong with them that a few days' rest won't cure. Incidentally, I'm quite glad to hide my total lack of eyelashes and eyebrows behind dark glasses." He touched her hand briefly. "It's wonderful to see you, Judith! Sit down and tell me all about everybody and everything. Melanie does her best, but she's just not interested."

So she sat down beside the bed and brought him up-to-date, first of all about Heather, explaining how ashamed she was at being the cause of so much trouble. Then she went on to describe how her father was coping with one wrist out of action and the group practice minus its most energetic doctor.

"Dr. Graham's been very good. He heard about the fire and insisted on coming back for a few days. They weren't far away – only at Duneham – and Dad's got Mrs. Dixon's eldest son driving him around. He was at home, out of a job, and luckily he's got a licence. Dr. Corder is doing a bit more than normal, but not much."

As Judith chattered on, she was suddenly aware of an odd sense of tension. Hugh was saying very little, but that wasn't the cause of it because she hadn't expected him to talk much.

Suddenly she faltered to a stop. "That seems to be all, I think. Is – is there anything else you want to know about?"

Hugh was silent for so long that she became panic-stricken. She had talked too much and tired him, or perhaps she had said something to annoy him though she couldn' think what it could be.

"I'm sorry – " She stood up uncertainly. "You're not really up to visitors yet. I'd better go now."

"No!" He reached out and seized her arm and there was nothing invalid about his grip. "Don't go, Judith – please. It was so wonderful seeing you come through that door. I've been lying here and thinking about you – "

His fingers slid down her arm and captured her hand, intertwining with her own, and Judith stood there – a prisoner, and wildly, incredulously happy because of her captivity.

She didn't know what it meant – it couldn't really mean anything at all – but it was wonderful all the same.

And then Hugh told her what it meant.

"I keep re-living over and over again that terrible moment when you went upstairs at the cottage with the roof blazing over your head. I made myself a promise then, but I didn't know when I'd get a chance to keep it."

He paused, not so much for a reply but to think out what he was going to say. When he began speaking again his voice was very slow and deep.

"I understood then that I loved you more than I'd ever loved anybody on earth, or ever would, and I knew that I must tell you so, no matter what the outcome might be. And so I *am* telling you, my dearest love, but – but I can't go on while you just stand there and say nothing. I know it's all very sudden and the last thing you expected, but just tell me that you don't hate me – *please*!"

Judith's eyes had been fixed on their clasped hands but she raised them now. She still couldn't really be sure that she had heard aright, but there was a wild exultation pounding through her veins in spite of it.

"You want me to tell you that I don't hate you? Oh, Hugh, of course I don't!" She sat down on the bed, heedless of the possibility that a nurse might come in, and leaned towards him.

With an abrupt gesture Hugh tore off the dark glasses. His eyes, red-rimmed and sore, gazed up into hers and in them she saw the birth of incredulous hope.

"You didn't ask me if I loved you," she said gently, "but I do, my darling – so very much. I think I have right from the beginning, but I didn't realise it either."

"Oh, Judith – " Emotion threatened to overwhelm him. "I didn't think it was possible – I can still hardly believe it." He struggled to take her in his arms. "Oh, damn these bandages!"

Judith kissed him on the lips – carefully because of the burns. She longed to pillow his poor damaged head against her breast, to pour out her love and make plans, but there was something which must be cleared up first.

So, after a moment, she asked quietly: "What about Melanie?"

"Melanie?" Hugh sounded utterly bewildered. "I'd certainly appreciate some help with her, of course, but – "

"Not that. I – I thought you loved *her* – I mean, I did until a few minutes ago. I even understood that you might be going to marry her when she's old enough."

"*What?*" He sat bolt upright in his amazement. "Naturally I love Melanie, but how could I possibly marry her? She's my niece."

"She told me she was adopted, so she's no relation really."

"The devil she did!" There was anger in his voice now. "There's not a word of truth in it, Judith. You've got to believe that."

"But why should she make it up?" she demanded as waves of relief washed over her. "It seems so – so unnecessary."

Hugh shrugged. "Who can tell? But she does tend to live in a fantasy world, you know, and I expect it seemed more interesting to imagine herself an unwanted baby."

It also meant that she could invent a romance between herself and Hugh, but Judith said no more about that. The information she had just received had made her so wildly happy that she could feel no animosity towards Melanie at all.

"I think most of the village heard the story," she said. "And they didn't approve of you two living at Birch Cottage while Mrs. Crowfield was away. It'll have to be put right."

"But how?"

"For Melanie's sake, let's wait till she's gone back to school – it won't be long now. And then I'll have a word with Mrs. Dixon; that ought to spread it round the village pretty quickly."

"It would certainly be the kindest way to do it – not that the naughty girl deserves kindness!"

"I think she does," Judith said gently. "She's still suffering from the tragedy that happened earlier in the summer."

"You're right, of course." His clasp on her hand tightened. "But don't let's talk about it any more. They'll be turning you out soon and we haven't got anything settled. When will you marry me, darling? Please, please let it be soon!"

"Just as soon as ever you like," Judith told him steadily.

Their lips met again, as gently as before, but they both knew that there would be plenty of time in the future for a more passionate manifestation of their love.

Also available this month
in the Mills & Boon Doctor - Nurse
Romance Series

TROPICAL HOSPITAL
(The Palm-Thatched Hospital) – Juliet Shore

Dr. Christina Roberts, stranded by tropical rains and unable to reach her fiancé, is offered temporary shelter and a job by the dynamic Dr. Mount.

Can her engagement survive the twin hazards of a further separation and the relationship with her new colleague?

LOOK OUT FOR THIS TITLE AT YOUR NEAREST MILLS & BOON STOCKIST Only 50p